MW01178782

Plan B is
Total Panic

Brad
Merry Christmas /91

Love Dad
Mom Noel

MARTYN GODFREY

Plan B is Total Panic

James Lorimer & Company, Publishers
Toronto 1989

Canadian Cataloguing in Publication Data
Godfrey, Martyn
Plan B is total panic

(Time of our lives)
ISBN 0-88862-851-X (bound) — ISBN 0-88862-850-1
(pbk.)

I. Title. II. Series

PS8563.08165P58 1986 jC813'.54 C86-094414-X
PZ7.G62P1 1986

0-88862-850-1 paper
0-88862-851-X cloth

Cover Design: Dreadnaught
Text Design: Michael Solomon
Cover Illustration: ONI

The publishing company acknowledges the
generous assistance of Alberta Culture
towards the publication of this book.

**Teacher's guide available from publisher.
Write to address below.**

A *Time of Our Lives* Book

James Lorimer & Company, Publishers
Egerton Ryerson Memorial Building
35 Britain Street
Toronto, Ontario M5A 1R7

Printed and Bound in Canada

To my Aunt Elsie

CHAPTER 1

I guess I got attacked by a grizzly bear because Sandra Travis is one terrific dancer.

If I hadn't watched her dancing on the gym floor with her friend, Jeanne, everything else wouldn't have happened. But I couldn't help it. You see, Sandra dances better than any other girl in my grade seven class.

"Close your mouth Nicholas," a voice shouted above the music.

I turned to look at Elvis Ah-Kim-Nachie, a native kid in my homeroom.

"You've got your mouth open," he smiled. "If Sandra sees you, she'll get embarrassed."

I closed my lips. "Thanks," I said. Elvis was sort of my friend, although we didn't do a heck of a lot together. Our fathers worked for the same oil company. That gave us enough in common to eat lunch at the same table.

"This is an okay sock hop, huh?" Elvis said. "It's a good idea to have them every Friday lunch. You danced yet?"

I shook my head. There was no way I could ever go up to a girl and ask her to dance. I was strictly a spectator at sock hops.

"Sandra can really move it," Elvis observed.

"Yeah," I nodded. I had this fantasy where I imagined Sandra was my girlfriend. I thought about how neat it would be to have her write my name inside a heart on her binder. And I'd take her to the show and hold her hand. But I'd never, ever admit that to anyone.

It would be like committing suicide, because Sandra's real-life boyfriend is Gerry Walmsley.

Gerry Walmsley scared the spit out of me, though in a way I wanted to be just like him. He had lots going for him — good looks, sandy hair that kind of waved over his head. And he was tough.

I wasn't born with any of that stuff. My nose covers half my face, which wouldn't be so bad if it wasn't painted with freckles. My hair is the color of a rotting log, and it sticks out like the fur on those bushy guinea pigs.

But I always figured that if I had muscles and courage, being semi-ugly wouldn't be so bad. But I had missed out on those as well. Being born with spaghetti biceps hadn't done much for my image.

I guess I was sort of a wimp. I'd never been in a fight in my life. I did my best to avoid them. When I saw that someone didn't like me, I made sure I stayed out of his way.

Gerry didn't have to do any of that. All he had to do was strut down the hall with his head thrown back and stare at everybody. It drove the girls crazy.

A lot of kids thought they were right out of it unless they were hanging out with Gerry's group. Guys tried to suck up to him to get to be his friend. I wasn't his friend. As far as Gerry was concerned, I was a nothing.

The music stopped, Jeanne left, and Sandra stopped dancing. She started checking out the people standing against the walls. She looked at Elvis for a moment and then at me.

And then she smiled, a cute little Sandra Travis half-grin, and started walking toward me.

I shifted against the wall and felt a flock of butterflies beginning to party in my stomach. What was she doing?

I heard Elvis mutter something, but I wasn't sure what it was because Sandra came so close to me that I could smell her watermelon bubblegum.

"Hi, Nicholas," she said softly. "Do you want to dance?"

I stared at her.

"Close your mouth, Nick," she said. "Let's go."

I looked at Elvis. Somehow I couldn't believe that Sandra was actually talking to me.

Elvis grinned at me and nodded. "Go for it," he said.

"I can't," I told Sandra.

"Huh?" She looked angry.

"I mean, I can't dance," I explained.

Her smile returned. "There's nothing to it. Just do what I do." She grabbed my hand and pulled me onto the gym floor.

The next song blared out of the speaker and I started to imitate Sandra's moves as best I could. I got right into it.

I'd never danced with anyone before. I'd never even tried to do it at home when Dad wasn't there. I always thought that dancing would make me embarrassed. But it didn't. Shaking to the music and being close to Sandra was fun. Yeah, I was definitely getting into it.

4

It wasn't until the song was half over that I realized what I was doing. I was dancing with Gerry Walmsley's girlfriend!

I looked at her and she smiled at me. "You're doing great," she called.

I looked at the other dancers. They'd made a circle around Sandra and me. A couple of the guys were giving me "I'm-glad-I'm-not-you" looks.

Then I glanced back at Elvis. He was smiling and shot me a thumbs-up sign.

I searched the darkness of the gym for Walmsley. I couldn't see him. Maybe he wouldn't know what I had done. Maybe nobody would tell him.

I began to back away from Sandra, hoping that I could ooze off the dance floor, but Sandra took my hand again and tugged me back. This time she didn't let go. I pulled at her grip and she twisted around in a circle, doing one of those old dance steps.

"Hey?!" I knew the voice before I turned around.

Sandra released my hand. "Hi, Gerry," she said. "Where have you been?"

"Around," he said as the music faded out.

Gerry was leaning his weight on one leg and had his thumbs tucked in the belt loops of his jeans. His head was tilted slightly, as

5

if he was trying to understand something terribly difficult.

I felt my knees begin to shake. "Hi, Gerry," I croaked.

"Now isn't this cute?" he said, casually brushing his hand through his hair.

"Gerry, don't start with that ... " Sandra began.

Gerry held up his hand to stop her. "Hey, this has nothing to do with you. This is between me and Nicholas."

Sandra rolled her eyes and Gerry returned his attention to me.

"Nicholas," he said. "You know, I always thought you had a lot of smarts."

"I'm sorry," I muttered.

"See?" He grinned and threw his arm around my shoulder. "See, you do understand, don't you? You were dancing with Sandra, and you know that Sandra and I are going out. Everybody knows that, huh?"

I nodded.

"Gerry, I asked him," Sandra broke in.

He raised his eyebrows. "Then we'll have to discuss that later. Now, I'd appreciate it if you didn't interrupt Nicholas and me again. Okay?"

Sandra sighed.

Gerry began tapping my shoulder. "Nicholas," he started shaking his head as if he was really sorry. "I'm going to have to pound on you."

"But I don't want to fight," I pleaded.

"Don't do this to yourself," he said sympathetically. "Let's get it over with. Come outside." He pulled at my shirt.

"Please, Gerry," I begged.

"Hey, Nicholas," he leaned close to me and whispered. "Everybody is watching us. If you don't come now, what are they going to think?"

"Leave him alone," Elvis moved beside me. "He didn't do anything. It was just a dance. You've got him scared enough."

"Butt out, Elvis!" Walmsley snapped.

Elvis might have guts, but he was no match for Walmsley. Nobody was. That's why I couldn't go outside with him. He'd kill me.

Another song blasted from the speakers. Gerry swore. He began to shout above the music. "Look, Nicholas, if you don't come with me I'm going to have to pound you here in front of everybody. And then I'm going to have to get you later as well."

I started shaking my head. "Gerry, please ..."

He looked at the people who had formed a wide circle around us. Then he shrugged and punched me right in the centre of my nose.

7

A softball of pain grew in the middle of my face and a river of warmth flowed across my lips and chin. My eyes filled with tears as I dropped to the floor.

I was aware of a chorus line of bright blue dots performing inside my eyes. I knew I was on my hands and knees and I knew there was a puddle of red forming on the floor beneath my face.

But for a few moments, maybe longer, everything else was fuzzy. I heard the excited voice of Mr. Gagesch, the gym teacher, but I had no idea what he was saying.

Then I recognized Elvis's voice. "Are you all right, Nicholas? Try to stand up."

Arms pulled me to my feet and I staggered while the gym reeled into focus.

"Holy ... " someone called. "Look at all the blood."

A couple of kids gasped.

"Are you okay?" Elvis asked again.

"No," I said. The taste of blood made me gag, and the gym heaved again.

"Elvis, Marcus, give me a hand getting him to the washroom." Mr. Gagesch was giving instructions. "Let's stop that nosebleed. Then we'd better take him over to the doc."

"We're still going to fight," Gerry Walmsley called to me. "We've only just started."

8

I focused on him standing behind Mr. Gagesch. The gym teacher whirled around. "I told you to get to the office!" he snapped. "Now move it!"

Walmsley stared at the teacher. Then he smiled and hooked his thumbs in his belt loops and swaggered toward the gym doors. A couple of his buddies followed at his heels.

"It's all right, Nicholas," Elvis was telling me.

I looked at him and nodded as salty tears mixed with the bitter taste of my blood.

CHAPTER 2

HALF an hour later I was sitting on an examining table in the emergency room of the High Level Hospital. Dr. Raghbir was gingerly touching my nose and looking very serious.

"Good, good. It's not broken, Nicholas," he said. "But it should be. You took quite a punch." He reached for a Kleenex. "Here. Wipe your eyes."

I did as I was told. The doc had a way of making everything seem like it was under control. I'm not sure what it was about him, but I think it had something to do with his voice. It was so smooth. And he said some of the words funny, so sometimes when he spoke it sounded like he was reading a poem.

"Does it still hurt very much?" he asked.

I shook my head. "No, it's just a dull throb now."

The doc pulled a chair from the corner and sat down. "I've got a little time, Nicholas."

I first started being friendly with Dr. Raghbir last spring. My dad made me join minor league softball in May because he felt it would be good for me to compete against other kids. What he really meant was that he hoped it would make me more aggressive. But it turned out all right, because Doc Raghbir was my coach.

Heaven knows where he got the time. Being one of two doctors in the whole of northwest Alberta is a twenty-four hour job. Not only does he take care of High Level, but he's always flying himself into the neighboring towns and settlements to do his rounds. I guess he figured coaching kids was part of his civic duty or something.

Doc Raghbir wasn't the greatest softball coach. He didn't know much about the game. Most of his coaching tips were "Go get 'em" type comments. Of course, no one blamed him, since he was from Bombay, India, and had only been in Canada for four months.

Part of the deal of moving to Canada was that he had to spend six months working in the boons. When his half year was up, we expected him to head for the city. But he

11

didn't. He stayed. Just that fact made him one of the most popular people around.

"I like it here," he told me once. "There's so much space and so few people. It could be warmer, though."

The doc always found time to talk to me. After the games, he'd take me aside and ask how things were going. We'd talk about my dad. And my mom in Calgary. And all sorts of stuff that I wouldn't even discuss with my father.

"I have a few minutes," he said again. "I'm flying to Rainbow Lake in a little while, but if you want to talk ..."

I wiped my eyes again. "I just wish things were different, that's all."

"What are you talking about?"

"My life," I sighed. "My whole life. I just wish I wasn't such a complete jerk."

I thought he was going to interrupt and tell me not to be so hard on myself, but he waited patiently for me to go on.

"Doc," I continued, "I've lived in nearly every oil town in the north. I've been in Peace River, Grande Prairie, Fort McMurray, Cold Lake, Rainbow Lake. You name it, I've probably lived there."

"To some people that would sound quite interesting," the doc said.

"It's the pits," I snarled. "I've never had a place to call home. Even now, Dad is talking about going to the Middle East, for cripe's sake!"

"It's warm there," he smiled.

"I know what you're trying to do," I said. "You're going to let me rave on about how lousy all those places are and then you're going to tell me that every place has something good about it and that I should look for that."

He chuckled. "You know me too well. That's exactly what I was trying to do."

"Doc, sometimes there doesn't seem to be *any* good at all. It's been the same everywhere I've lived. Each time I start a new school, I get pegged as a wimp. And it's true."

"I don't think so," he said. "There's a saying about people making something come true because they believe it."

"But everybody at school believes it," I pointed out. "Did you know that in every single town there is at least one guy like Walmsley?"

"Really?"

"Yeah. Every new school that's built gets a Gerry Walmsley."

The doc smiled. "What does your father say you should do, Nicholas?"

13

"Dad's idea about the whole thing is simple. You punch out the other guy's lights before he punches out yours."

The doc scratched his forehead. "I've always thought that if two people fight, it proves nothing, except that one is stronger or more vicious than the other. I think you're right trying to avoid fighting."

"Thanks, but what happens if you can't talk your way out of it?"

"You run away." He nodded to himself. "You run away so I don't have to take care of your nose."

"But I can't run," I told him. "My legs get like rubber and I feel as if I'm going to throw up."

"Feeling afraid is normal."

"But my fear is more than normal," I explained. "I'm scared. Scared out of my mind. I'm afraid to go back to school. Walmsley says he's going to beat me up again. And I know he'll do it."

The doc was nodding his head slowly. "Nicholas, I've got to fly myself to Rainbow Lake now. But we'll figure out a way to deal with your problem without getting into another fight. Why don't I call you at home when I've finished my rounds this evening? Maybe you can drop by my office when I'm doing my files. How does that sound?"

"You don't have to do that … " I began.

He held up his hand. "Hey, Nicholas. It is not what I have to do, but what I want to do."

I smiled. "Thanks, doc."

"It's all right. Now I've got to get to my plane."

I felt my swollen nose. "I'm going to go home and change my shirt. I'm not going back to school today."

Doc Raghbir stood up and handed me my jacket. "I'll call you when I return from Rainbow."

"Okay." It was nice of the doc to try to help, but I figured I'd need more than his advice to get me out of this one.

I went home, threw my bloody sweatshirt into the garbage and spent the rest of the afternoon watching TV. I was able to lose myself in this movie about a robot from the future chasing someone's mother so the son wouldn't be born to revolt against robots. It sounds stupid but I loved it. I wished I was just like that cyborg. Boy, would Walmsley ever get a surprise when he tried to punch me and I ripped his guts out.

Around four o'clock, someone knocked at my door. I checked out the window to make sure it wasn't Walmsley. Elvis Ah-Kim-Nachie waved at me through the glass and I let him in.

15

"Hey Nicholas," he said, looking at my nose. "I was thinking about you all afternoon. I wondered how you made out at the hospital."

"Fine," I said. "Considering that my nose is twice as big as it usually is."

"Yeah," he nodded, "I noticed. That's too bad, because you got a big nose to begin with."

"Thanks," I said as we went into the kitchen. I offered Elvis a can of Pepsi and we sat at the table. "How's Walmsley?"

"Gerry's terrific," Elvis said. "He's strutting around telling everybody that he's going to finish discussing things with you this weekend."

"That makes me feel better," I moaned.

"I think he expected you to come back to school," Elvis went on. "When you weren't there at 3:30 he looked disappointed."

I groaned. "I'm in big trouble."

"You sure are," Elvis agreed. "But not till tomorrow. Tonight Gerry and the group are having a party at Sandra's."

I sipped nervously at my drink.

"But ... " Elvis paused to take a long swallow of pop. "But tomorrow, I wouldn't be surprised if you're Gerry's project for the day."

I sighed.

"Which is why I came over here, Nicholas."

"What?"

"Your dad is working this weekend, right?" Elvis asked.

"Yeah," I said. "He'll be home tonight, but tomorrow he's doing double shift and he's going to stay at Zama overnight."

"My old man, too," Elvis told me. "You and me got a lot in common, huh?"

We had a few things. Both of us lived with our fathers. Both our parents were divorced. Both our mothers lived in different places. My mom was remarried and living in Calgary. His mom was living on his reserve in Chateh.

But we had a lot of differences as well. Elvis liked to spend his free time in the bush. I couldn't stand it. But more important, Elvis wasn't a wimp.

Those were enough differences to keep us from being close friends.

"Look, Nicholas," Elvis explained, "I don't want to spend the weekend in town. And I figured you'd probably appreciate the chance to get away as well. So I'm off to my reserve tomorrow to go moose hunting with my grandparents. You want to come?"

I stared at him for a few moments and then shook my head. "No, thanks. I couldn't kill anything, especially something as big as a moose."

17

"Come for the trip then. We're going down to Hay Lake. It's really pretty there."

"Thanks, but no. I don't really like being out in the bush. There's too many bugs and things."

"Bugs?" he laughed. "This is October. The frost has killed them off. This is the best time of year. Warm days, cool nights, no bugs."

"I'm not that type of person," I muttered.

"What are you babbling about?" Elvis asked. "Just come with us. You don't have to do nothing except enjoy. What would you do here? You couldn't even go outside."

"But ... "

"But nothing." Elvis thumped the can down on the table. "I'm trying to be your friend, stupid. Don't turn me down."

I looked at his big round face and the equally big smile that grew on it as he watched me. I sure could use a friend.

"Okay," I said.

"Great!" Elvis chuckled. "We'll have a good time, I promise. Just bring a change of clothes. Your dad won't mind, huh?"

"I'll ask him about it when he gets home, but I doubt it. He'll probably be thrilled. He's been trying to get me to go hunting with him for years. He figures it'll make me tougher."

"You could use that," Elvis nodded. "My uncle is in town tonight. He'll be driving to

18

Chateh at eight in the morning. We'll pick you up then."

As I watched Elvis walk down the street, I was sorry I had agreed to go. I wasn't sure I wanted to spend a weekend in the bush. Even to get away from Gerry Walmsley.

CHAPTER 3

JUST as I thought, Dad started beaming when I told him that I was going to go moose hunting. He slapped me on the back and tried to convince me to take his rifle. But there was no way I'd do that.

We ate Hamburger Helper for supper and then he left for the Legion. Dad spends most of his nights with the guys in the Legion lounge. Sometimes he'll go there right from work and I'll only get to see him at breakfast.

I spent Friday night watching TV, worrying about Gerry Walmsley and waiting for Doc Raghbir to call. He didn't, which kind of bothered me because I really needed to talk to someone. But I knew how busy he was and that he'd get back to me as soon as he could.

The next morning I packed a bag and waited for Elvis. He was an hour late.

"I thought you'd never get here," I grumbled as I climbed into the back seat of his uncle's beat-up car. "I was just about to phone you. You said eight."

Elvis was sitting in the front seat. He twisted around to speak to me. "Close enough. You knew what I meant."

"Close?" I searched for a seatbelt. "You're an hour late. I could have slept in."

"Dene time," he said. "Natives have a different sense of time."

"Don't give me that," I mumbled as I felt under my backside for the belt.

"Your nose looks better," he said.

"Thanks, but I still feel like I'm wearing a grapefruit on my face."

"May I ask what you're doing?" Elvis asked, puzzled.

"Looking for a seatbelt."

"Ain't none, man," came the voice from the driver's seat.

"Oh, I'm sorry," Elvis apologized. "Nicholas, this is Uncle Harvey."

"Nice to meet you," I said.

"Call me Wild Dog." Harvey turned around, grinned with an infectious smile and shook my hand. He wasn't very old, no more than twenty. "All my friends call me Wild Dog."

"Interesting," I said. "An unusual nickname."

"Uncle Harv got it when he was just a kid," Elvis explained. "He has these fits."

"Fits?"

"Like when I was just a little guy I fell off a roof and hit my head. Don't remember what I was doing up there, but I do remember my perfect headstand — straight down," Harvey told me. "It did something to my brain. Every so often I have these fits where I bounce around and stuff. And I kind of howl. Like a dog. That's how I got the name. But they don't last long."

"You ever get these fits while you're ... um ... driving?" I asked.

"Not yet." Harvey pulled the gears into drive. There was a grinding noise followed by a thud. The car lurched into motion.

Not yet? "Why aren't there any seatbelts?" I asked.

"I don't know, man," Wild Dog said. They weren't in when I bought it."

"Relax," Elvis told me. "My uncle is a great driver."

"Right," Harvey declared. "I ain't had an accident since I drove into that tree in September."

I sighed. Maybe it would have been better to stay in town and face Gerry Walmsley.

"Stupid place to put a tree," Uncle Wild Dog laughed.

It wasn't until we turned onto the dirt highway that linked High Level to Rainbow Lake, 125 kilometres away, that I noticed the windshield was so full of stone chips and runs that you could barely see out of it. And Uncle Harvey was charging along so fast that I half expected to pass into warp speed.

"Aren't you going a little fast?" I asked.

"Naw," Harvey disagreed. "I could drive this road with my eyes closed."

I looked at the window again. "I think that's what you're doing."

"You ever been out this way?" Elvis asked.

"Fishing once with my dad. But we didn't go as far as the reserve."

"Fishing? I thought you hated camping and stuff."

"I do," I said. "My dad had been bugging me for months to go out and get some jackfish. I finally said yes so he'd leave me alone. It was a disaster. I caught this big pike and Dad wanted me to bash it on the head to kill it. I wouldn't and we ended up arguing. He told me how much of a disappointment I had turned out to be. Then he drank beer for the rest of the afternoon.

"We'll make sure nothing like that happens this weekend," Elvis promised.

"Thanks," I said. "To tell you the truth, I'm not all that excited about hunting and killing something."

"You don't like to hunt, man?" Wild Dog spoke up.

"I'd rather be sailing," I said.

"Huh?"

"A bumper sticker," I explained.

"Huh?"

"Nothing."

"I like to hunt," Wild Dog nodded. "Yeah, nothing like going into the bush to kill something. Hey, you wanna hear something funny?" He chuckled. "We got this cousin called Earnest."

Elvis started to laugh. "This is really funny, Nicholas."

"Well, Elvis's dad and Earnest went out after a moose one day," Wild Dog went on. "They found these tracks in the muskeg and split up. About half an hour later, Elvis's dad hears this rustling in the bush and figures it's the moose. So he blasts it. And guess what? It was Earnest."

Both Elvis and his uncle broke out into loud laughter.

"That's not funny," I protested.

"The bullet hit him in the bum," Elvis explained between guffaws. "Blew a hole in his right cheek."

"That's not funny," I said again. "How can you laugh at that?"

"Every time he sits down now, he leans to the right," uncle Wild Dog howled.

"He could have been killed," I said seriously.

Elvis wiped at the tears in his eyes. "You're not laughing, Nicholas."

"I think that's an awful story," I explained. "Earnest could have been really hurt or killed."

"But he wasn't," Elvis said. "I mean, it he was hurt, then it wouldn't be funny. But since he wasn't, it is."

I stared at him.

"No, huh?"

I shook my head.

"Oh, well," Elvis sighed. "It must have something to do with our cultures. I don't really find Gilligan's Island that funny. You *egeeyah* are always laughing at stuff that makes me shake my head.

"Egeeyah?" I asked.

"White people," Elvis told me. "Since you're going to spend the weekend on the reserve, I'm going to have to teach you some Dene. Turn you into a real Native."

"I have enough trouble with French."

"Ah, but Dene is easier. It doesn't have as many words. Now you take *Dene.* That means person. It also means The People. Same word."

"Convenient."

"*Edekle* means paper," Elvis continued. "So what do you think *edekle dene* is?"

"Paper person?" I answered.

"Right. That's what we call a teacher."

I smiled. "I guess it fits."

"Now, *koa* is house, so an *edekle koa* ... ?"

"A paper house," I answered. "A paper house is a school?" I was getting into it.

"You got it," Elvis nodded. "Now *chine* means stick, so an *edekle chine* ..."

"Is a paper stick, which has to be a pencil."

"You sure your mom wasn't a Native?" Elvis grinned. "You're catching on real fast."

"You eat beaver?" Wild Dog interrupted.

"Pardon?"

"Beaver. You like to eat beaver?" Uncle Harvey repeated. "Elvis's grandmother made up a big pot yesterday. Maybe it'll be still on the stove if you want some."

"You don't really eat beaver, do you?" I scrunched up my face. "Those things are rodents. They're related to rats."

Elvis began laughing again. "I've got a feeling I'm going to really enjoy this weekend."

I'm glad someone is looking forward to it, I thought, as I watched the spruce and poplar blur past the side window.

I think one of the reasons I had always disliked the bush was that there was so much of it. When I thought about how small the towns I had lived in really were and how enormous the wilderness was, it scared me.

Most Canadians live so close to the southern border, they don't realize how much of their country is still wild — the great white north. There's something about it that makes you feel small.

When I had told my dad that, he just said, "When did you start thinking crap like that?"

After an hour, we turned off the dirt highway onto a narrower and more potted gravel road.

"This is the boundary of the reserve," Elvis told me. "There used to be a sign, but Uncle Harvey drove into it and knocked it over."

"That was last year," Wild Dog said defensively.

As we rounded a curve, I saw an RCMP 4X4 parked on the road. There was a cop beside the truck waving us down.

"You're not carrying, are you?" Elvis asked his uncle.

Wild Dog shook his head. "Naw, I gave that up. Neither of you are, huh?"

"Get real," Elvis said.

"Carrying what?" I asked.

"Booze," Elvis explained. "Chateh is a dry reserve. That means it's against the law to have alcohol. The cops often search cars coming in."

Wild Dog braked the car with a shrill squeal. He wound down the window as the officer approached us.

The cop bent over and looked into the car. "Hi, Harvey," he said. "Hey Elvis, how are you? I haven't seen you for a couple of months. How's it going?"

"Good," Elvis replied. "Sergeant Jarvis, this is a friend of mine from High Level, Nicholas Clark."

Sergeant Jarvis looked at me and smiled. "Nice to meet you."

"You looking for beer?" Wild Dog asked.

Jarvis shook his head. "Not this time. We're trying to find a missing plane and we're stopping everybody to ask if they've seen anything."

"What missing plane?" I asked.

"Dr. Raghbir's Cessna from High Level," the cop told us.

"Dr. Raghbir!" I gasped.

The cop nodded. "That's right. The doc was in Rainbow Lake doing his rounds yesterday afternoon."

"I was with him," I said. "Just before he left High Level, I was talking to him in the hospital. What happened?" I couldn't believe that the doc's plane was missing.

"We don't know," Jarvis shrugged. "Dr. Raghbir left Rainbow Lake at sunset. He never showed up at High Level. There was probably enough light for him to follow the highway back to town."

"Do you think he's … " I didn't know what to ask. "Do you think he's hurt or … "

The cop looked at me. "Sounds like you're a friend of his."

I nodded and he gave me a brief smile.

"I'm sorry," Jarvis went on. "We have no idea what happened. He didn't radio about any trouble. If he was following the highway and had problems, he should have landed on the road. If he went down out of control, the plane shouldn't be far, either, but we've been flying search planes and nothing has turned up. At this time we just don't know."

"We ain't seen nothing," Uncle Harvey said.

Jarvis nodded. "Well, it goes without saying that if you see anything at all, get in touch with us right away."

"You bet," Elvis said.

Then Jarvis pointed at the windshield. "Look, Harvey, I've warned you about fixing this thing. Next time you go to town, get a new windshield. If you don't, I'm going to have to give you a ticket and impound the car."

"Okay," Wild Dog said. "I'll do that."

"I'm serious, Harvey," the cop said firmly. Uncle Harvey nodded.

"Take care." Jarvis waved us on.

Uncle Wild Dog had the car up to light speed in a few seconds. We roared into the townsite. I sat back in the seat feeling a little stunned. The doc — missing! It seemed unreal. I was just talking to him less than a day before. Now he could be hurt. Or even dead.

"This is my reserve," Elvis interrupted my thoughts as we tore through the settlement.

I looked at the wood-frame houses and wondered who had planned the layout. It was like somebody had shuffled the houses and dropped them from the sky. Some were so close that you'd be able to hold hands through the windows, while others were planted in the middle of fields. Some faced the road; others were sideways and a few were backwards.

The car veered to the right and plowed along a pot-holed dirt driveway. Again it screeched to a stop.

"This is it," Elvis called out. "Grab your bag and let's go."

As I climbed out of the car I looked at the house and squinted. It was such an awful colour, kind of like blueberry bubblegum.

"I may see you later," Wild Dog said to us as we got out of the car. Then he threw up a cloud of dust as he sped down the driveway.

"He's a nice guy, huh?" Elvis smiled.

"Just terrific," I agreed as I looked around the yard.

There was a lot of yard. It was covered with ankle-high brown grass and twelve or so spruce trees.

There were a couple of dogs tied to a small tree to the right of the house. They looked at us with mild curiosity but didn't bother to stand up and bark.

Just beyond them was an outhouse. The door had been painted with a terrific portrait of a Native wearing a buffalo horn headdress. The character's arms were folded over his chest, revealing comic book muscles. There was a tattoo on one arm saying, WE'RE NOT GONNA TAKE IT.

"That's impressive," I said.

"Uncle Harv did it," Elvis told me. "He's got quite the talent."

I looked on the other side of the house. There was a tepee there. Thin aspen saplings had been leaned together and covered with burlap and plastic. "What's that?" I asked.

31

"A tepee."

"That's what I thought."

"Are you okay?" Elvis asked. "You're acting like you're in a fog."

"I'm sorry. I guess I'm just a little shook up about Dr. Raghbir."

"That's a bit of a shock, huh? But I've got a feeling everything will turn out all right."

"I sure hope so," I said. Then I pointed at the tepee. "Do you sleep in there?"

Elvis laughed. "Good grief. It's used as a smokehouse. We smoke meat or the hide inside."

"Smoke it?"

"Oh, boy," Elvis was shaking his head. "To preserve it. Smoking dries it out so it doesn't go rotten."

"Oh," I nodded.

"Yeah, oh," he mimicked. "Come on. Let's go in the house."

The inside of the house was painted the same awful colour as the outside. It was so dark that my eyes were still adjusting to the light when a little girl popped in front of us. She couldn't have been more than seven.

"My step-sister, Agnes," Elvis said.

She started speaking to Elvis in Dene. He listened, nodding his head and adding an occasional "*ah*." Then he made a mock frown

32

and pretended to slap at her rear end as she ran away giggling.

"Agnes says that my mom isn't here. Mom has a job as cook at one of the lumber camps. She works for seven days straight and then gets a week off. She just started her shift, so I guess you won't get a chance to meet her."

"That's too bad," I said.

"And Agnes also says that you look like a *gon cho*."

"A what?"

"A *gon cho*. It means big skinny."

"Big skinny?! I'm not sure I ... OW!

"You can't meet my mom, but you can meet my grandmother." Elvis grinned.

I turned around gingerly. Elvis's grandmother had a tight fistful of my hair. "Ow!" I protested.

The old lady stared at me from behind a wrinkled and leathery face. Then she broke into a toothless grin and spoke rapidly in Dene.

"Could you let go of my hair, please?" I pleaded.

She started to laugh and nod her head, but she didn't let go.

"This really hurts," I protested again.

Elvis spoke to her and she released my hair and clapped her hands a few times.

"She likes your curly hair," Elvis told me.

I rubbed at my scalp. "Does she want it?" I grumbled.

"Are you making fun of my people?" Elvis pretended to be angry.

"*Yu huh,*" a deep voice called from the doorway.

I glanced over the shoulder of Elvis's grandmother and saw an elderly gentleman. The old lady walked to the door and they both left the house.

"That was my grandfather," Elvis said. "He has the wagon loaded and we're all set to go. Leave your bag on the coach and let's go get the family a moose."

"Fine," I agreed.

"Agnes," he called. "Norma!" Agnes came out of the bedroom followed by a younger girl. She was about five and smiled at me as she darted by.

"My other step-sister," Elvis explained as he went to a wall-mounted gun rack and picked a bolt-action rifle. "It's a .306, kind of old, but it still works. We got another .30-.30 if you want to take it."

"No, thanks," I shook my head. "Those things scare me."

"Sure hope we don't run into the grizzly, then," Elvis mumbled.

"The what?"

"Well, we're going hunting near Hay Lake," he told me. "Last week Thomas Talley said he saw a big grizzly down there. He said it was a monster of an animal."

"Bears are afraid of people," I said.

"Not grizzly," he said seriously. "Grizzly will come looking for people."

"You're kidding, right?"

He tried to keep the serious look, but then he broke into a broad grin. "Yeah, I 'm putting you on, *gon cho*. Bears avoid people like we avoid them."

"That's what I thought," I said as I walked out the door.

"Yeah, they sure do avoid people." Elvis closed the door behind him. "Most of the time."

CHAPTER 4

ELVIS helped me into the back of an old wooden wagon and introduced me to his grandfather. The old man regarded me with a stony expression for a few moments and then turned his attention to the scragglylooking horse hitched to the front. He gave the reins a sharp whip, and the horse began to trudge across the yard toward a path into the bush.

"This is a shortcut to Hay Lake," Elvis explained. "There's some muskeg along the way, and it's too narrow for a car. The wagon is the perfect way to go."

"I'll take your word for it," I said as the wagon rode a bump and bashed my back into one of the sideboards.

"Sit right against the boards," Elvis suggested. "That way you won't bounce so much."

I shuffled against the grey pitted wood. "This wagon is pretty old, huh?" I asked.

"No idea," Elvis said. "Been around as long as I can remember."

"Does your grandfather always use a horse?"

Elvis shook his head. "No, if he needs to get into High Level, he'll catch a ride with Uncle Harvey. He only uses the wagon when he goes hunting. And that's only a few times a year. The horse is almost wild. Most of the time it runs loose in the fields. If Grandad wants it, he has to chase it. Sometimes it takes him a box of sugar cubes and the whole day to get a bridle on." He laughed, and called in Dene to his grandmother. She was sitting with her arms around the two girls. She started to laugh as well.

"My grandmother has always said that she doesn't know who is more stupid — my grandfather for letting the horse run loose, or the horse for not running away into the bush."

I smiled and glanced at the trees that made a roof over the trail. They were poplars, and since it was mid-October, they had all lost their leaves.

But the sun was warm and it shot laser-like beams through the patterns of branches. I could almost appreciate why some people liked to camp. Almost.

It had been a great autumn. We'd had some snow in early September, but then it had warmed up. The days were getting shorter in a hurry and that was something I could do without. Going through the winter with four hours of sunlight can get you down. I always wondered how the people who live in the far north put up with twenty-four hours of darkness.

"Nice, huh?" Elvis asked.

I nodded. "Can I ask you a question?"

"Sure," Elvis answered. "As long as I don't have to answer."

"Why is your house that colour?"

"That's the colour my grandfather asked for. The houses are shipped up in parts from Calgary. We get to choose the colour. It's super, huh?"

"Just super," I lied.

"Yeah, High Level is so boring," Elvis grumbled. "You *egeeyah* always want to paint your houses that off-white colour."

"No taste," I agreed. "By the way, how come the houses aren't in rows? They seem to be all over the place."

"That's another thing I don't understand about High Level," Elvis confessed. "You've got to build your houses on those skinny little pieces of land. On the reserve, you find a place you like and you have the house built there. If you want to be alone, fine, put your house in a field. If you want to live right next to your parents, you can do that, too. It's a much better way."

"But what about the water pipes and the sewers? How do you service the homes?"

"We don't have running water or sewers," he said. "So it's no problem."

"You don't have water in your house?"

"Don't look so stunned," he smiled. "You can't miss what you've never had. We carry water from the creek and use an outhouse. Remember that picture Uncle Harvey painted? That was the door to our only toilet."

"I don't think I could live like that," I said.

"Yeah, I agree," Elvis laughed. "You're too soft."

I ignored the insult. Why argue? It was true, anyway.

I thought about the doc. My dad never went to church, so I hadn't got into the habit, either. But I kind of said a prayer for Dr. Raghbir. I hoped that he was all right.

I'm not sure how long it was before the wagon drew gently to a stop.

"Hay Lake?" I asked.

Elvis shook his head and put his finger to his lips. He watched his grandfather reach behind the wagon seat and throw aside an old blanket. Beneath the cloth was a pump-action, .12 gauge shotgun.

"Does he see a moose?" I whispered.

Elvis made a puzzled face. "With a shotgun?" he whispered back. "Ducks. There's a marsh over there to the left. We have to get our lunch. Follow grandfather."

The old man jumped spryly from the seat, walked in front of the horse and then vanished into the bush. Elvis climbed over the sideboard and hopped to the ground. I imitated his move a little less nimbly. The old lady gave me a wide gummy smile.

About twenty-five metres into the bush, we found his grandfather squatting behind a patch of tall grass. Elvis quickly dropped to one knee and pulled my jacket to get me to do the same.

The old man gave me another stony stare, pointed over the grass and nodded twice. Then he bounded to his feet and charged forward.

Elvis jumped up just as quickly and I stumbled after them. Soon I was walking through wet peat and the water squished into my running shoes. I was looking down at the swampy mess to get a better footing when I ran into the back of Elvis. As I staggered to regain my balance, grandfather shot three rapid blasts.

The thunderous noise made me twist away. I lost my balance altogether and fell into the wet bog on my hands and knees.

I looked up at Elvis. He was trying not to laugh. At least, he tried for a few seconds.

"You sure are a happy guy," I said sarcastically.

He grabbed my arm and pulled me to my feet. "You looking for ducks down there?" he chuckled.

His grandfather appeared through the tall grass and regarded my wet clothes. I expected him to laugh as well, or at least to smile, but he didn't. He stared with the same hard expression, shook his head and marched back toward the wagon.

"Your grandfather ever smile?" I asked.

"Oh, sure," Elvis nodded. "He doesn't really like *egeeyah*, though. He figures you guys don't know anything about the real world, which to him is the bush."

"I guess I'm making a good impression then," I said as I began to follow the old man.

"Where you going?" Elvis asked.

"Huh?"

"We've got to get lunch." He jerked his head and began to walk through the grass.

I reluctantly followed, heading farther into the marsh. We came to a growth of rushes and a decent stretch of pond. In the centre of the water floated the bodies of four dead ducks.

"Only four," Elvis remarked. "He usually gets more. My grandfather is a great shot. He waits until they're just taking off, when they're all bunched up. And then — bang — a whole feast."

I stared at the poor birds in the pond. "How are you going to get them?" I asked.

"Not just me," Elvis grinned. "You and me. How are *we* going to get them."

"Okay, how are we going to get them?"

"Easy. We're gonna wade out there."

"We're going to what?"

Elvis sloshed through the reeds toward a mound of grass that was growing on some deadfall. He stepped up and pulled off his wet sneakers and socks. Then he took off his shirt.

"You're kind of wet already," he noted, "but unless you want to be completely soaked, you'd better take off your clothes before you go any deeper."

"What?" I grunted intelligently.

Elvis pointed at two of the ducks that were drifting to the left. "You get those two." And then he dropped his jeans and underwear and started wading toward the other two birds. "Let's go!" he hollered.

I splashed toward the mound and took of my shoes and socks. I wasn't up for this. "Can't you make two trips?" I suggested.

"That isn't fair," Elvis called. "Besides, you've got to prove something to my grandfather."

"I don't care what he thinks," I said. "I have no pride. Remember, I'm out here because I'm running away from Gerry Walmsley."

"Don't be a total wimp," Elvis teased. "This is a once in a lifetime chance. Think what you'll be able to tell Sandra Travis." He was up to his waist now and closing in on his ducks. "Come on. It's fun."

I sighed, pulled off my jeans and stood shivering in my jockey shorts. "I'm not really doing this," I said. "I'm not really stripping off so I can go skinny dipping in a muskeg swamp."

Elvis turned to look at me. "Way to go. You're almost there."

I nodded dumbly, removed my shorts and marched into the pond. The water was so cold that an explosion of goose bumps appeared on my skin. As I went deeper, I began to shiver violently. And then I hit the slime.

Northern lakes are so cold and the summer is so short that the dead plants and leaves that end up on the bottom don't get a chance to decay. Instead they form an oozy, muddy layer of organic mulch.

The stuff squashed rudely between my toes. I sank down to my ankles and as I wrenched my feet free a stream of bubbles drifted lazily from the gunk and burst on the surface. A heavy rotten odour surrounded me.

I swore loudly for the benefit of Elvis who was moving back toward his clothes with a duck in each hand.

"Be careful," he called. "The bottom is a little soft in places."

"A little soft!" I shouted. "I'm walking in a sewer!"

He looked at me as if he didn't understand why I was complaining.

Still shivering, I moved slowly toward the ducks. I ripped up great quantities of underwater muck. Large, odorous bubbles burst around me.

I had a flash thought of all the things that lived in the muck that clung so wonderfully to my feet. All sorts of slimy worms and multi-legged bugs must have been checking out my toes.

By the time I reached the ducks, the water was past my navel.

I recognized the birds from science class as being two male mallards. I grabbed their green necks and gratefully turned around.

By the time I slogged back to the mound, Elvis was almost finished dressing.

"That wasn't so bad, was it?" he asked.

"Tell me about it," I grumbled as I dropped the ducks on the grass and climbed the deadfall.

I dressed quickly, grabbed the mallards, and headed to dry ground. "It'll take me years to get warm. Do you do that a lot?"

Elvis nodded. "Only in the ponds. On the lake I usually go after them in a canoe."

"There has to be a better way than walking through the muck," I complained.

Elvis frowned. "Why are you upset? You're going to eat the birds, aren't you? You just helped out. Grandfather shot them. We retrieved them. Norma and Agnes will clean them and grandmother will cook them. Everybody does a little."

"Not what I meant," I said.

"Different lifestyles, huh?" he smiled.

"I guess," I agreed. "I'd rather go to McDonald's."

45

"I went there once when I was in Edmonton."

"I'll have a McDuck with cheese," I joked. "Hold the pickle."

Elvis stared at me, completely dumbfounded. Then he shrugged and headed back toward his family.

We handed the ducks to his grandmother. She kneaded them and smiled, obviously pleased with their plumpness.

"Where are the girls?" I asked.

"I don't know," Elvis shrugged.

At that moment, Norma and Agnes came darting out of the bush from the same direction as the pond. They hopped up beside the old lady and began to giggle.

"They were watching us." I said. "They were watching us when we went for the ducks."

Agnes whispered into her grandmother's ear and the old lady looked me up and down and began to laugh.

"They were watching us when we had our clothes off, why ... " I felt my face redden.

"They didn't see nothing they haven't seen before," Elvis said as he climbed into the wagon.

I hoisted myself behind him and snarled at the girls. Then I sighed. I had a sudden picture of my warm living room, a bowl of popcorn and the movie channel. What was I doing here? Surely facing Gerry Walmsley couldn't be worse than this.

CHAPTER 5

It was past noon when the bush trail stopped and we found ourselves at the shore of Hay Lake. Grandfather turned the wagon north and followed the shoreline until the spruce turned into willow and then the tall grass. We continued to hug the water until we came to a growth of aspen forest.

"There was a lot of rain early this summer," Elvis told me. "Usually, the shoreline is way out there. I can remember one summer when the lake vanished. Just a few wet spots left."

"Must be a pretty shallow lake," I said.

"It's not really a lake," Elvis explained. "More or less a big marsh. A wildlife officer once told me that there are more kinds of water birds here than any other place on earth."

The old man pulled on the reins and the wagon eased to a halt. Elvis hopped over the sideboards and I followed.

"Let's get some firewood," he called as he started toward the aspen growth.

"It's pretty out here, Elvis." I watched a slight wind ripple the water. Above, high wispy clouds stuccoed the sky.

"Yeah," Elvis agreed. "You should see it in September. There's so many ducks and geese. Canadas, Snows, even a few swans. And cranes, they land on the dry spots. It's almost unbelievable that there are that many birds."

"I'd like to see that."

"You would?" he asked.

"Sure."

"Maybe there's hope for you yet," he smiled.

We reached the aspen and began to pick up deadfall for the fire.

"Elvis, do you mind if I ask you another question?"

"You want to know how come I'm so good-looking?"

I laughed. "Actually, I'm curious about your name. How'd you end up with a name like Elvis?"

"I suppose it is unusual, huh?" he thought. "My mom named me Elvis. She has this thing for the dead singer. She's got all his old records and she keeps sending away to the States for these junky Elvis souvenirs. Did you know he was part Native?"

I shook my head. "That's neat. My mom has a thing for the Beatles. I'm lucky I didn't end up being called Ringo."

"That sounds like an okay name," he said seriously.

By this time we had gathered hefty armfuls of wood.

"This is a good place for moose." Elvis changed the subject. "Lots of young plants. Just what they love." He waved his foot at a mass of brown, grape-sized pellets on the ground.

"What's that?" I asked.

"Moose droppings," he told me.

I laughed. "I'm not that stupid, you know. A moose is a big animal. When it does a dump, it doesn't leave those little things."

"Sure it does," he said as we returned to the wagon. I gave him a knowing wink.

"Those are moose turds," he insisted. "How long have you been living in the North, Nicholas?"

"All my life. I was born in Peace River. Edmonton is way down south to me."

Elvis shook his head. "For a guy who's lived near the bush for so long, you sure don't know much about it."

"I know enough," I told him.

"You really think … " he began. "Holy … Nicholas, look at this! Look!"

Elvis chucked his bundle of firewood and dropped to his hands and knees. I threw my load to one side and squatted beside him.

"Look at that!" He pointed to a large indentation in the earth.

The depression was an animal track, fairly round with several pointed claw marks.

"What made that?" I asked. "A bear?"

"Not just a bear, friend. A *gleeze*."

"A what?"

"A *gleeze* . A grizzly."

I looked around nervously. "How do you know that? How do you know it isn't a black bear?"

He pointed at the claw marks. "Grizzly have their claws out all the time. Just like that. A black bear can pull its claws in, like a cat. The marks don't show in the tracks. Besides," he spread his fingers and placed his open hand in the tracks. There was room for another hand. "It's too big," he went on. "No black leaves a print this huge. It's got to be a *gleeze* ."

I twisted around. I half-expected to see a grey-brown monster charging from the trees.

"The tracks are fresh," Elvis announced. "They were probably made this morning when it was cooler." Then he looked at me and grinned. "Neat, huh?"

"No," I said quickly. "I find it scary being in a place where there's something that could eat me." I picked up my pile of firewood. "Maybe we should head back to your family where the guns are."

Elvis looked at the line of trees. "Good idea," he agreed. "A rifle would definitely help. I told you to bring that .30-.30 along." He picked up his load of deadfall and we marched back to the wagon.

His grandfather was sitting cross-legged on the ground and we dumped the firewood in front of him. I sort of expected the old guy to start a fire by rubbing two sticks together. Instead he reached into his shirt pocket and pulled out a ball of plastic wrap. Inside was a cube of white stuff. It was barbecue starter.

He placed it on the ground, lit it with a match and began to arrange the wood. Within minutes there was a roaring fire.

While the old man had been starting the blaze, Elvis had been speaking to him in animated Dene. The word *gleeze* had been repeated frequently.

By the time the fire had started, Grandfather's face was bubbling with as much excitement as his grandson's.

Elvis stood up. "Grandfather says it would be a great thing to kill such a bear, but he says we must be careful."

My mouth dropped open. "You're kidding?! You're not seriously thinking about going after a grizzly bear. You'd need a tank."

Elvis shook his head. "No, I'm not thinking about going after it. Grandfather would never allow it, anyway. But there's no harm in hoping we run into it while we're chasing the moose, is there?"

"I can see a lot of harm in that."

He stared at me and grinned. "I got you going, huh? The *gleeze* isn't anywhere near here by now. If he was, we'd scare him away."

"But you said ... "

"Yeah, what are you going to believe?"

"Elvis ... " I began, but I was interrupted by Agnes and Norma carrying a duck each. "*Chi*," they giggled as they sat next to the grandfather.

The old lady followed behind with the two other ducks. She sat with a mournful groan and threw one of the ducks to me. I fumbled with it for a few moments before holding on.

I stared at the lifeless body. "What am I supposed to do with this?"

"Grandma says that she'd like to see the *egeeyah* clean the *chi*," Agnes grinned.

"Clean it?"

The girls giggled.

"Clean it?" I asked again.

"Gut it," Elvis explained.

"Gut it?"

"Boy, are you slow catching on," Elvis said. "Grandmother wants you to take the guts out."

I looked at the duck again. "You want me to pull the insides out? You want me to pull out all those intestine things?"

"That's right," Elvis nodded.

"You're afraid," Agnes piped in. "You're afraid of the insides."

"No, I'm not," I lied.

They continued to giggle. So what? I wasn't going to pull out the insides of a dead bird just to prove something to a couple of little kids.

"Don't do it if you don't want to," Elvis said. "It's girls' work, anyway."

"Pardon?" I looked at him. "What do you mean?"

"Just that it's usually the girls who do the cleaning and stuff."

"You shoot them; they clean them. That doesn't sound fair."

54

"I guess it isn't," he agreed. "But that's the way it is. Guys only help if they really want to."

"Are you afraid of the insides?" I teased.

"Course not."

"You want to clean it?"

He stared at me and then at the duck. "No, thanks."

It was my turn to give him a knowing smile. I sat down next to the grandmother and said. "*Egeeyah* clean *chi* ."

The old lady gummed at me and began to pinch balls of feathers from her bird's body. I imitated the action and immediately regretted it. A duck louse leaped from the bird onto the back of my hand. I jumped and swatted madly at the little bug.

"They can't hurt you," Elvis said. "They only live on ducks."

What was I trying to prove? I didn't want to debowel a mallard. Just the thought made me feel nauseous. But I felt the need to prove something to Elvis and his grandparents.

The old lady offered me a bloody knife and pointed to the duck's stomach.

"Stick it in, huh?" I asked.

"Not quite," Elvis said. "You cut from the rear end to the breast bone. But don't go too deep. If you rip the intestines, you'll ruin the bird and it'll stink."

55

"Great," I complained. "It sounds like surgery."

I made a jagged cut across the bird's stomach. I was surprised at how much force I had to use to cut through the muscles. When I was finished red and blue things quivered at me.

"I can't do it," I confessed.

Grandmother made her hands form a scoop and began to nod her head rapidly.

"You want me to stick my fingers in and pull that yucky stuff out?"

Even though she didn't understand English, it was obvious that she knew what I meant, because she continued to bounce her head and gum at me.

I looked at the guts and moaned. Then I turned away, stared at Elvis with gritted teeth and thrust my hands into the bird's body.

I wish I could say that I bravely finished the job, but as soon as the semi-warm intestines oozed between my fingers, my stomach decided to try to journey up to my throat. I swallowed hard and stood up. "I've got to go for a walk," I said as I strode away from the campfire.

A chorus of laughter accompanied me.

Elvis jogged beside me. "You okay, Nicholas?"

I swallowed again, feeling only slightly better, and nodded.

"I didn't laugh," Elvis told me. "I think that was sort of a brave thing to do."

"Thanks." I tried to smile. "I guess I made a big impression, huh?"

"On me, you did," Elvis smiled. "I always thought you were a bit of a wimp."

"Thanks a lot," I snapped.

"It's true. You've always avoided things that make you feel uncomfortable. You don't join the other guys and mess around. And the reason you're here is because you're afraid of Gerry Walmsley. Sticking your hand in a duck's guts is a big breakthrough for you."

"I'm doing stuff I never thought I'd do," I confessed. "I mean, wading in that pond and trying to gut the duck."

"Way to go," he encouraged.

"But the thing is, I knew I wouldn't like doing them and I was right, so why did I do them in the first place?"

"Just because you've got to test it out to know for sure," he offered.

I began to feel better and took a couple of deep breaths. We walked around the wagon and returned to the campfire.

I was pleased to see that the old lady had finished cleaning my duck. She dragged the bird thought the fire a few times to singe away the pin feathers and then cut the bird along the spine. She poked the duck on a pointed stick that Grandfather had sharpened and propped it near the fire.

"It'll take an hour until they're done the way my grandfather likes — burnt black," Elvis told me. "Let's go look for a moose."

I glanced at the trees. "Do you think it's safe to go in there with a grizzly bear around?"

"We've been through that," Elvis grumbled. "Bears are afraid of people, remember?" No smart grizzly is going to hang around when it smells people."

"What if it isn't a smart bear?" I asked.

"Hey, I'd love to see the *gleeze* so that I could shoot it," Elvis explained. "But there isn't much chance of that. Besides, we aren't going to walk into the trees. We're going to scout around the outside of the bush and try to scare the moose back this way. Right toward Grandfather."

"I don't know." I shook my head.

Elvis picked up his .306. "Let's go."

I followed a step behind him, anxiously looking over his shoulder to see if something big and hairy was waiting for us.

CHAPTER 6

ELVIS snapped the ammunition clip into the rifle when we reached the edge of the tree line.

"This is great, huh?" Elvis declared.

I looked apprehensively into the aspen trees, still not convinced that Elvis was telling the truth about bears being afraid of people. "I'm not sure," I answered.

In the distance, to the north, a small aircraft droned lazily across the blue sky. It was so far away that it was merely a black dot.

"I guess they're looking for Dr. Raghbir," I said, pointing at the plane.

Elvis searched for the dot. "Probably," he agreed. "It looks like it's following the highway."

"It's kind of weird, huh? I mean, what could have happened to him? If he crashed, he couldn't be far from the road."

"I don't know," Elvis shrugged.

"I sure hope he's okay."

"You're pretty close to him, huh?"

"He was my softball coach," I replied. "I mean, look how busy he is all the time, and he still found time to talk to me. We talk about things that I don't tell anyone else. Like ... things about how I feel about my parents' divorce and living with my dad."

"You get along with your old man, don't you?"

"Yeah, I guess so. But he's never home."

"Hey, I can understand that. My old man works overtime two, three times a week," Elvis told me.

"But even when my dad is home, he's not. He spends most of his time drinking with his buddies in the bar."

"You mean he drinks too much?" Elvis asked.

"I don't know. But he always has a can of beer in his hand."

"Sounds like it," Elvis nodded knowingly. "I had another uncle who drank so much he ended up in the hospital with a bleeding stomach. Crazy, huh? You ever talk to your dad about his drinking? You ever tell him that it bugs you?"

I shook my head. "You don't talk to Dad about stuff like that. That's why I talk to Dr. Raghbir."

"Well, look," Elvis said. "If you ever need someone to hash things out with, give me a holler. And I'll do the same, okay?"

"Thanks. Although ... " I paused.

"Although what?"

"Well, if I ever told you something personal, you'd probably tell the whole school."

"No, I wouldn't."

"Oh, yeah?" I smiled. "What about that time that Tom Kinkson told us that he still sucked his thumb when he was sleeping and his parents were making him sleep with mitts on. Remember that? And remember Tom asking us not to tell anybody else?"

"I didn't just tell *anybody* else," Elvis said. "I told Joanne, that's all."

I laughed. "Telling Joanne is like having it broadcast on the news."

"But I didn't do it on purpose. I felt sorry when the kids started razzing him," Elvis confessed.

"Sure you did," I teased. "I'll think twice before I tell you personal things."

He chuckled. "Hey, Nicholas, you ever have a girlfriend before Sandra Travis?"

"Sandra Travis?" I smiled. "I should be so lucky."

"Well, you ever have a girlfriend?"

"This counts as a personal area."

"You can trust me," he smirked. "Answer the question."

"Sort of," I said. "In grade five. I was in Grande Prairie then. There was this girl called Shannon."

"Nice name."

"We used to mess around together."

"Mess around?" He raised his eyebrows.

"Knock it off. You know what I mean. I took her to the show a couple of times, watched the videos at her place, stuff like that."

"You ever kiss her?"

"What?"

"Don't be so thick," Elvis grinned. "Did you ever kiss her?"

"Once," I confessed. "At a birthday party. Well, actually it was more than once, but it was only one time. I mean, I didn't kiss her any more than that once, but it was more than once."

"Huh?"

"I mean, some of the kids were dancing and I kissed her a few times then," I tried to explain.

"Was she pretty?"

"Yeah," I nodded. "In a way, but she had a strange nose. It was kind of peeled back, so when you were looking into her face, you were looking up her nostrils."

Elvis wrinkled his forehead.

"But the thing I really liked about her was that she could burp something fierce."

"She could burp?"

"Lay one down that would make the walls shake."

"Cute," Elvis nodded.

"We used to buy her Pepsi and she'd drink it fast and let it rip. You wouldn't believe it."

"And you could see up her nostrils?"

"I remember that every time we had a substitute teacher, Shannon would spray out a horrendous belt from her desk. *ARRRRRPPPPPPP!*" I tried to imitate the noise.

"Sounds terrific," Elvis laughed. "I figured you'd have a girlfriend like that."

"Like what?" I asked.

"A girl who could outbelch the whole province and had look-and-see nostrils."

I punched his arm. "Watch it!" I tried to sound angry. "At least I had a girlfriend."

"I've got one now."

"Where?" I scoffed. "I haven't seen you hanging around with anybody."

"She's not in High Level," he told me. "She lives on the reserve. Her name is Rachel."

"Nice name."

"She's really cute," he smiled. "Got long hair all the way down to her waist. We used to hate each other when we were little kids. Funny how things change, huh?"

"You ever kiss her?"

"Sure," he boasted. "Lots of times."

"Come on."

"Well, a few times," he corrected. "She really likes me. Everyone calls her *Bagula*."

"What?"

"*Bagula*. That's her nickname, just like yours is *Gon Cho*."

"What's it mean?" I asked.

He scratched his chin. "It's kind of hard to say in English, but I guess it means Chubby Cheeks."

"Chubby Cheeks?"

"Yeah. She has a round face."

"Chubby Cheeks?" I said again. "And you were making fun of my belcher?"

"It's a nickname," he protested. "It's a compliment. When we give people nicknames, we're complimenting them."

"Oh, yeah?" I snapped. "And what about *Gon Cho*? Don't tell me that Big Skinny is a compliment?"

"Sure it is. In a way it tells everybody that you're an individual, worthy of a special name."

I laughed.

"We have a guy on the reserve whose name is Bear Claw," Elvis went on.

"Because he's got a hairy hand?" I continued to laugh.

"Naw, because he was attacked by a bear."

I stopped laughing.

"Yeah, he was chased by a big black who ripped up his face and head. He's got these great blue scars over his head."

"That's awful," I said. "That's worse than the story about Earnest. Doesn't he get upset when everybody makes fun of his scars?"

"Of course not. Those scars are a status thing. How many guys do you know with claw marks over their face?"

"None," I answered.

"See? That's why he doesn't mind."

I shook my head trying to figure that one.

"So *Gon Cho* is a nice thing to ... " Elvis stopped and looked at the ground. He dropped his voice and pointed at an indentation in the grass. "Great."

"Great what? You don't see another bear track, do you?" I thought about how Bear Claw had got his name and swallowed.

He nodded. "You hear anything?"

65

"What do you mean, do I hear anything?" My stomach was tightening into a knot.

"I mean this track is fresh. Real fresh. So don't talk so loud."

"Let's head back," I suggested quickly.

He shook his head. "No way. We are real close and downwind. This is perfect."

"Perfect for what? You said that you wouldn't hunt the thing."

"I know," Elvis grinned. "But I didn't say anything about tracking it so I could get a good look at it."

"That's stupid!" I snapped.

"Ssssh." He made a stern face. "You might scare it away."

"Good. You don't go tromping through the bush with the idea of following a grizzly bear."

"Stop being so ... so ... you," Elvis scolded. "When was the last time you saw a grizzly bear?"

"In the Calgary zoo. And it scared the pants off of me then."

"Nicholas," he cajoled. "This is the chance of a lifetime. Seeing a big *gleeze* in the wild. Watching it for a few minutes. It's a story you'll tell forever."

"I'm going back."

"Fine," he said. "But remember you've got no gun."

I stared at him. "What does that mean? Does that mean you think I could run into the bear?"

He shook his head. "No, I don't mean that. I just don't want you to miss this chance. Look, I know we're all right here. I know you'll be okay walking back to my grandparents without a rifle. I'm just trying to tell you that it'll be no problem to track the bear. And if there is, I've got the rifle."

"I don't know."

"Come on," he coaxed. "Trust me. If you can't trust a Native in the wilderness, who can you trust?"

"You sure?" I was beginning to give in.

"I'm sure," he nodded. "Come with me."

"You're not going to try and hunt it? You promise?"

"Well ... "

"Promise!" I insisted.

"Of course I won't hunt it," he said. "Let's go for it, huh?"

"Okay," I muttered, not quite believing I had said it.

He checked the direction of the tracks and moved into the bush. "Don't worry," he said. "We've got a gun."

"And a bear has four clawed feet and lots of teeth," I reminded him.

"You're still talking too loud."

As we entered the poplars, the trail became easy to follow. The bear had literally bulldozed its way though the underbrush. The wild rose bushes and saplings had been flattened.

We plowed farther into the trees and I began to feel a deeper sense of dread. "I'm sure this isn't a good idea," I whispered.

"Sssssh!"

Suddenly, there was a loud screeching noise to the left. I nearly jumped out of my skin as a squawking whisky jack flew between the branches.

My legs were shaking so much that I had to support myself against a tree and suck in deep breaths.

"Stupid bird," Elvis croaked.

I looked at him. "You okay? Your voice is kind of shaky."

"Yeah, I'm fine," he continued to croak. "It's just that the bird made me jump."

I nodded. "I know the feeling."

"Come on," he snapped impatiently.

And so we went further into the forest. "I don't see anything ahead," I observed, hoping that Elvis would call off the chase and return to the idea of hunting a moose.

"We'll go on."

The trail led to the lake. Elvis pointed at the tracks near the shoreline. "Stopped here to drink."

He did the same, kneeling by the water and scooping handfuls of the clear liquid. He grinned at me. "This is good for me, you know. There's something in me that feels at home doing this. I can get the feeling of how my ancestors lived."

"I bet your ancestors didn't follow a grizzly bear," I grumbled.

"This is my heritage," he went on. "Part of my culture. Can't you understand that?"

"I can understand that you're proud of being Dene, but I don't think two kids following a grizzly bear is part of your heritage."

"We're not kids, you know," he said. "To the Dene, we're all grown up now. Once you've hit twelve, that's it."

"You're putting me on."

"No, it's true. There are even a couple of girls our age who are already living with guys. Starting a family. Different cultures. Your whole view of the world is different. Take hunting. The *egeeyah* will take a 4X4 into the bush and start tromping around until they find something. If it's dark and they haven't killed anything they figure they've wasted the whole day. But a Dene will head out into the bush, find moose

69

tracks and sit down and wait for the moose to come back. If it takes two days or five, it makes no difference."

"I'm not sure which way is best," I told him.

"But the *egeeyah* teachers try to teach us their view. That's why it doesn't work. That's why most Native kids drop out in junior high."

"But you've got to get ready for the real world," I pointed out.

"Hey, if you were stuck our here in the bush for a week, would you know how to survive?"

I shook my head.

"Well, this is the real world, too." He made a tight smile and then followed the trail back into the bush. I scrambled after him.

Ten minutes later, the thick bush began to thin into willow thickets dotted with aspen saplings. Tall grass grew between the small trees and it was easy to follow the path flattened by the grizzly.

The ground began to rise and we left the poplars behind. The willows grew stunted and the grass was shorter. Large patches of hard brown dirt polka-dotted the ground.

Elvis stopped and peered down intently. "I've lost the tracks," he grumbled, kicking at the caked dirt. "This stuff is like cement."

"Great," I smiled. "Terrific news. Let's head back."

He gave me an angry look. "It's like the *gleeze* vanished," he complained.

"Oh, well." I couldn't help smiling. "Maybe next time, as they say."

He propped his rifle against one of the small willows, reached into his jacket pocket and removed a can the size of a hockey puck. It was snuff — ground up tobacco.

"You want some?" Elvis asked.

I shook my head. "No, I didn't know that *you* used it."

"I don't very often," he said. "Oh, I used to when I was living on the reserve, but when I moved to High Level, I cut down. The teachers don't exactly like you spitting in school. You ever to try some?"

"No." I watched him twist the lid and pop a small piece deftly under his bottom lip.

"Try it." He offered the can to me.

"No, thanks."

"If you don't like it, then spit it out."

I looked at the blackish-brown substance. I figured I had just been tracking a grizzly bear. If I could do something that stupid, then I could try a pinch of snuff. A weekend to do wild things. I reached over and pinched some between my thumb and forefinger. "Just tuck it in, huh?"

Elvis nodded and peeled back his bottom lip to reveal the mass resting beneath his teeth.

I placed the tobacco against my gum. Immediately a bitter, foul liquid seeped around my tongue, stinging the sides of my cheeks. My mouth started to water profusely and I swallowed a large mouthful of tobacco saliva. It stung the back of my throat and made me gag.

"Good, huh?" Elvis grinned.

I tried to say something, but my throat tightened up and tears dripped from my eyes. And then a wave of nausea hit me like a hammer. The grassland began to heave and reel and I had to plant my feet apart to keep my balance.

"Great, huh?" Elvis was chuckling. "Just like you felt the first time you saw Sandra Travis."

I spat the vile mess out. "I'm all dizzy."

"Yeah, it always does that the first time. After a few times, you'll get used to it."

The landscape slowly stopped swaying.

I groaned and shook my head.

Elvis was laughing. "You definitely look a little green," he teased. "No kidding."

"You keep laughing and I'm going to puke on your jeans," I threatened.

"I'm sorry, but you really do look ... " He stopped, frozen, and stared over my shoulder. There was a slight shaking to his lower lip. I twisted around. Thirty metres behind me was the largest animal I had ever seen.

The grizzly was a monster, far bigger than anything I had ever imagined. Its presence filled the environment. The creature's head seemed hideously large. The body was massive, an immovable tank. Its legs seemed as solid as mature white spruce.

The bear stood on all fours, staring curiously at us. It raised itself on its haunches, standing straight, and sniffed our scent.

I croaked out a string of swear words and turned back to Elvis. He stood, saying nothing, staring at the huge animal.

"The gun," I muttered. "Get the bloody gun!"

He didn't move. He didn't even look at me. His eyes remained focused on the beast. His bottom lip was shaking violently.

"Elvis!" I tried to shout. He still didn't move or say anything.

Somewhere the back of my mind was telling me, "He's frozen, Nicky. Your friend is so scared, he can't move. It's like the stuff you read about in books. You get so frightened that you can't do anything."

The bear snuffled and then snorted. As if in slow motion, it eased itself to all fours and began to jog. At first its steps were slow and lazy. But as it got closer, it increased its speed. The animal peeled back its lips, displaying long yellow teeth. Then it charged straight toward us.

CHAPTER 7

T HE gun!

I glanced at Elvis. He was staring blankly at the approaching beast. I charged past him, pushing him out of the way, and scrambled for the rifle.

"You've never fired one of these things," my mind spoke. "How are you gonna shoot the bear when you've never even had a sling shot before?"

The bolt, I thought. I had to pull the bolt to put a bullet in the barrel.

"That's right!" my mind cheered. "Got to get a bullet in there, Nicky, baby."

I pulled the bolt and heard the shell slide into the magazine.

The monster lumbered gracefully forward. It was a giant now, blotting the horizon. My gaze was drawn to the wide mouth. The teeth seemed to grow as the thing drew closer. Honey-thick saliva dripped from its lips.

"So, shoot it!" my mind ordered.

I whipped the rifle to my shoulder and tried to look through the scope. All I could see was out-of-focus, brown-grey fur.

I squeezed the trigger.

Nothing.

The safety, I thought. Before the rifle will fire, I have to flick the safety.

"Where the hell is it?!" I shouted out loud.

The bear was no more than fifteen metres away now. It was all I could see, a rippling, charging mass of animal.

Ten metres.

I couldn't see anything. No catch, no knob, no switch. I couldn't find the safety.

Eight metres.

"Play dead!" My mind sought frantically for an escape.

Six metres.

"Scream at it!" my mind howled. "Scare it away!"

The bear's black eyes seemed to drill into me.

"Run!"

Five metres.

Suddenly, the rifle was ripped from my hands. I stared at the charging grizzly, but out of the corner of my eye I saw Elvis raise the rifle to his shoulder and pull the trigger. The thwack of the bullet smashed against my cheek and deafened me. A violent spray of dirt exploded in front of the *gleeze* .

The animal yowled in surprise and snapped its head to the left. Incredibly, the body followed the head and the bear ran past us and back toward the trees. Cries of pain trailed behind it.

My legs felt like jelly. I looked into the trees to make sure that the thing had really left us. Then I looked at Elvis.

"Thanks," I finally croaked. "You saved our lives."

He stared at me, but didn't say anything.

"The bullet sprayed dirt in its eyes," I went on. "A faceful of dirt threw it off. You couldn't have shot any better if you'd hit it between the eyes."

The fear seemed to flow out with each word. I had to keep talking.

"You're so white, I could call you an *egeeyah*," I observed.

Elvis looked at me with a mixture of shock and shame. "I'm sorry," he mumbled.

"You're sorry for saving my life?"

"No," he shook his head slowly. "I'm sorry I was so scared. I froze, Nicholas."

"Me, too," I pointed out. "What do you think I was doing when you pulled the gun out of my hands?"

"Lots of big talk, huh?" he went on. "I talk tough about hunting the grizzly, but when I saw it I turned into a coward."

I watched the trees. Now that I was beginning to come down form the sheer terror, I started to think about the possibility that once the grizzly had recovered from the surprise of an eyeful of dirt, it might come back.

Then I stared at Elvis and sighed heavily. "Look, Elvis," I said. "I think I know how you feel." Of course I did. My legs were shaking so violently that I had to concentrate on standing still.

Again I glanced into the bush.

"The way I figure it, Elvis," I continued, "is that seeing a bloody monster in front of you can throw you off for a second or two."

"I'm a coward," he moaned.

"No," I tried to explain. "When that thing was breathing in our faces, when it was so close that we could count the hairs in its fur, you stepped in the way and shot it. When it really counted, you moved. And I owe you for that."

He looked into my eyes, took a deep breath and shuddered. "Thanks," he whispered.

Soon a stream of tears rolled down his cheeks. He didn't bother to wipe them away. And then my failing legs decided that enough was enough. I melted to the ground.

It took us half an hour before we pulled ourselves together enough to begin walking back to camp. We didn't say much to each other. I asked Elvis to show me where the safety was and he pointed to a tiny button behind the trigger guard. He asked me what I thought would have happened if his shot hadn't been so lucky. I just shrugged, refusing to think about it. And a couple of times we wondered aloud if the *gleeze* would come back.

Other than that, we simply sat and let our bodies return to normal. I don't know what Elvis thought about, but I didn't really think about anything. My head just numbed out.

We trudged around the edge of the trees, even though the journey would take us longer than cutting through the bush.

"My dad is going to have a bird when I tell him what happened," I said. "He'll call me a jerk for following a grizzly bear."

"You were," Elvis agreed. "But only half the jerk I was."

"What do you think Gerry Walmsely would have done?" I asked.

"Probably filled his pants."

"Do you think guys really do that?" I wondered.

"Sure," he said. "I remember this girl in my grade four class who wet herself when she got up to say her public speech to the class."

"I can't see Walmsley ever doing that."

"Would be funny, though," Elvis smiled. "But you're right. Gerry is too cool."

"He'd probably invite the bear to step outside."

"Especially if it had been dancing with Sandra," Elvis pointed out.

Then, in a half-decent imitation of Gerry Walmsley, I said, "Okay, you bear. I saw you looking at my girlfriend. I'm sorry, but I have to take you outside and rip your fur off. You can growl all you want, but I still have to pound you."

Elvis laughed. "I'm feeling better," he confessed.

"Me, too," I agreed. "It's kind of hard to imagine that what happened really happened."

"No, it isn't," Elvis disagreed. "I'll remember that moment for the rest of my life. I'll remember being stuck like a statue while a half tonne monster came at me."

"We could have been dead for a half an hour by now," I observed.

"Boy, you think some happy thoughts. No wonder you don't have any girlfriends outside of belchers."

We rounded a thick outcropping of trees and changed direction to the east. The aspen grew thick and wiry, bunched together with the competing balsam and poplar saplings. It was too thick to travel though. I regarded the bush gratefully. At least the bear wasn't in there.

"You know what I was thinking about just as that bear was going to get me?" I said. "I was thinking about something I'd read years ago. I think it was in a booklet we got when we visited Jasper. It said that if you see a bear and it starts to run at you, you should holler and hoot and sometimes that'll scare the thing away."

"Sounds like it'll sometimes make it mad," Elvis noted.

"It also said that if you can't scare the thing away, then you should drop into a ball and play dead, that sometimes the bear will leave you alone."

"And sometimes he'll eat you," Elvis disagreed.

"I guess," I said. "But the weird thing is that I must have read that thing when I was in grade three. And I hadn't thought about it until the bear was spitting in my face."

"I suppose your head was flipping through all its memories to try to find something to help you. Like a computer search."

"That's what I was thinking. That's sort of neat, huh?"

"Sort of," he nodded.

I looked into the trees again. The growth seemed even denser. Well, that was just fine with me. "There's no bear in there," I pointed out.

But there was something else.

At first I didn't believe I'd seen anything. My brain didn't relate a flash of blue and yellow between the white-and-grey trunks as being unusual. It took a few moments for me to stop and peer through the trees.

Yellow and blue?

Elvis had continued walking, unaware that I had stopped. I had to call him back. He jogged to me with his rifle ready.

"You see the bear?" he asked nervously.

"No," I answered. "But look at that."

"There's something in there."

We approached the trees carefully and began to push our way through the thick growth. It was almost impossible to move at all. We had to crush and break many of the saplings to make headway. I got a couple of wicked scratches on my right cheek.

As we beat our slow path into the bush, we saw more yellow and blue. It was becoming more of an object rather than just colours.

"I don't believe it!" Elvis gasped.

"The plane!" I exclaimed. "It's Doc Raghbir's plane!"

CHAPTER 8

THE plane had plowed through the small trees, exposing a tangled line in the bush. Elvis and I smashed our own way through the saplings to the crash site. It took minutes to reach the plane. Or rather what was left of the plane.

One wing had been torn off and I could see it resting upright about ten metres away. The other wing was bent at an impossible angle to the fuselage. The plane's body was dented and scratched. The cockpit was buried under the uprooted and shorn aspens.

"Holy ... " Elvis muttered.

"No wonder they couldn't find him," I said. "He was way off course."

"He?" Elvis asked.

I looked at the shattered Cessna. "Oh, geez," I moaned. "Doc Raghbir's still in there, isn't he?"

I started pulling the broken saplings away from the front of the plane, but Elvis grabbed my arm and stopped me.

"What are you doing?!" I snapped.

He squinted his eyes a little. "Nicholas, maybe he's … maybe he's dead."

I stared at the tree-covered cockpit.

"Look at it," Elvis said grimly. "Are you ready to see him dead? What if he's all ripped up or something?"

"We gotta look," I told him.

"I don't think I want to see him dead."

"We still gotta look." I went back to pulling trees away. "Doc!" I shouted. "Are you all right?"

There was no answer.

It took five minutes of hard work and I was sweating under my jacket before I was able to peer through the smashed glass of the cockpit. I could see a body slumped forward in the seat, still supported by the shoulder belt. It was Doc Raghbir.

"Is he dead?" Elvis asked.

"I don't know." I pressed my face against the shattered glass. "Doc," I called. "Are you okay?"

The body didn't move. He looked awfully still. His face was covered with ribbons of dried blood and I couldn't see his chest move.

"He isn't moving," I told Elvis.

"Let's get some help," he suggested.

"No, wait a minute." With my elbow I began to beat at a small hole in the safety glass. In a little while I had widened it so that I could slip my arm through. "I'm going to touch him," I said. "I'm going to see if he's warm."

I heard Elvis groan as I reached into the cockpit and put my hand gently on Doc Raghbir's face. The blood wasn't dry. It was sticky and the skin was definitely warm.

"He's alive," I shouted.

Elvis rushed to my side and we began to rip at the branches. After a few hard yanks, we opened the dented door.

"What do we do now?" Elvis stared at the doc's unconscious body.

"I'm not sure, but I know what not to do and that's move him. Let the medic guys do that."

"He looks like he's hurt real bad," Elvis observed. "We should get help right away."

I nodded. "Go back to your grandparents and ride into the reserve and call the cops."

"That's gonna take a couple of hours," Elvis said.

"What else can we do?"

"Over that way," he pointed back out of the bush, "is the Zama Road. It's the access road to all the oil wells and rigs. There's always trucks going by on that. I can flag one down and get them to call in on the CB or their mobiles."

"Always trucks?" I asked.

"Yeah. I may have to wait a few minutes, but it won't be a couple of hours. If I run over there, I'll be at the road in twenty minutes."

"Go for it," I said.

"Okay, you take the gun just in case that bear is still around." He propped the rifle against the side of the fuselage. "You remember how to flick the safety?"

I nodded.

He smiled. "I won't be long, Nicholas. I promise." Then he began to thread his way out of the bush. A minute later he reached the clearing. He looked back at me once, and then left me alone with Dr. Raghbir.

I looked at the doc's ashen face. It was like Elvis had said. He was badly hurt. I noticed that the right side of his face was swollen and that his right eye was puffed shut. So what could I do for him while I waited?

I squeezed into the smashed cockpit and rummaged around for a first-aid kit, but found nothing. It wouldn't have been any use, anyway. What was I going to do, put a band-aid on his head?

"You're going to be all right now." I said out loud. "Yeah, my buddy, Elvis, has gone to get help."

A bank of clouds covered the sun, turning the bush dark and gloomy. Without the sunlight, the temperature dropped quickly and I shivered.

"I'm sure glad you're alive," I spoke to him. "I was really worried when I heard you'd gone down. I'm glad I found you. I think you really wrecked yourself. I just hope we're not too late."

A couple of chickadees checked out the plane and chirped excitedly before flying away.

"I guess the search planes would have started looking farther from the road in time. Maybe tomorrow."

I sighed, feeling silly talking aloud. But I didn't know what else to do.

"I think you may have one of those concussion things," I went on. "And that's why you're not conscious. You remember when we were playing the game against Manning and Martin got hit in the head with the softball?"

The doc didn't answer, of course. He lay so still that I had the sudden feeling that maybe he'd died while I was talking to him.

I touched his cheek again and then checked my watch. It was almost four. No wonder it was getting darker.

I returned my attention to the doc. "You remember that, don't you?" I went on. "Martin was standing there at first, checking out that girl in the bleachers, the one with the halter top that didn't halter all that much." I smiled. "Yeah, Martin was staring at the girl and the Manning batter hit a line drive right off his head. He dropped like a cement kite."

I glanced at my watch again. Elvis had to be close to the road by now. With luck, he'd meet a truck right away.

"Anyway Martin was out cold for a few seconds but he wanted to stay in the game. You wouldn't let him. You made him sit out and about half an hour later he started getting all sleepy. Remember? You took him to the hospital and told us that he'd had a concussion."

A wind began to blow the top of the trees and the clouds turned greyer as daylight faded. There was a hint of rain in the breeze, or maybe snow.

"This has been a weird day, Doc. I came out here to get away from a guy who threatened to bite my head off and then I almost had my head bitten off by a grizzly bear. You should have seen this thing. It was bigger than ... "

"Warer ... "

I stopped talking and stared at the doc. His head was tilted toward me and his right eye was open.

"You're awake," I gasped.

"Warer," the doc muttered again.

"Oh, geez, that's a good sign," I exclaimed. "Being awake is a good thing, isn't it?"

"Warer," the doc grunted.

"Warer?" I repeated. "Warer? I don't know what you mean?"

The doc seemed to be focusing his good eye on me. There was a glint of recognition. "Nic ... las?"

"Right," I said. "It's me, Nicholas Clark."

"Warer," the doc insisted.

Warer? I thought. What the heck is that? Maybe it was East Indian or something.

"Warer," the doc said again and licked feebly at his lips.

"Water!" I jumped. "You're saying you want a drink of water?"

Doc Raghbir nodded weakly.

"I don't have a canteen," I shrugged. "I don't have anything to drink." Again I squeezed into the cockpit and searched for a canteen or water bottle. The only thing I found was an empty can of Diet 7-UP.

"Listen, Doc," I said. "I'm going to go down to the lake and fill up this can. I'll only be a few minutes. You hang on, okay?"

He moaned.

The wind bit into my face as I stumbled back to the clearing. The clouds painted angry swirls on the horizon. I began to jog back the way Elvis and I had walked. If I remembered well, there was an area of sparse spruce a few minutes back.

Elvis had to be at the road by now. He must have flagged a truck and the cops would know. They'd probably send out a helicopter. Hopefully they'd be there by the time I got back with the water.

I came to the patch of swamp spruce. There were mangy trees covered with thick growths of caribou moss. As I headed into the trees, the ground turned soft and wet. That explained the lack of aspen. I was running through muskeg.

For some strange reason, I had a thought about Gerry Walmsley. I wondered what he was going to think when he heard that Elvis and I had found the doc. He'd probably say "so what" and punch out my front teeth.

The spruce changed to willows and I quickly found myself at the shoreline of the lake. I squatted by the water, thrust the can

91

under and watched the air bubbles speed to the surface.

The freezing water made me realize just how cold I was. I reached into my jacket pockets and put on my leather gloves.

"Hurry up, Elvis," I muttered. "I don't really know what I'm doing here."

Up until that time, I hadn't thought about the bear. It hadn't even occurred to me as I was rushing to the lake, that I was going back into the bush where the grizzly was. I was so intent on getting water for the doc that the *gleeze* had completely slipped my mind.

And so as I turned around I wasn't ready for what waited for me.

The bear.

It was resting on all fours, no more than ten metres away. Its head was cocked sideways, like a dog when it's trying to figure something out. In the gloomy dusk, the bear was probably having trouble seeing me. Its nostrils twitched as it tasted the air for my scent.

My insides seemed to drop into a clammy mess at the bottom of my abdomen. I sucked air in rapid breaths.

The voice in my mind was reawakened. "Well, Nicky, baby, there we are. In trouble again. And you left the gun back at the plane."

The bear's brown-grey pelt blended with the willows. It was hard for me to tell where the bear ended and the trees began. In the dim light, the monster seemed to have grown to a terrible size.

"Doesn't matter how big it is, Nicky," my mind was telling me. "The fact is, it's a lot bigger than you are."

Instinctively I began to back away. Cold water soaked my sneakers and crept up my calves as I entered the lake.

The grizzly raised its black snout and began to move toward the shoreline. It was hideously large, but it moved with such a graceful step.

I had walked at least thirty metres into the lake, but the water only washed beneath my knees. I looked at the bear and then at the pop can. There was something funny about trying to get away from a grizzly bear and holding onto a water-filled Diet 7-UP can.

"Ha, ha," my mind chuckled. "That's a real funny one, Nicky, my boy. Now exactly what are you doing?"

"Bears can't swim," I thought.

"Says who?" my mind questioned. "Where'd you hear that?"

"Bears are afraid of water," I reasoned to myself.

"Sure they are," my mind protested. "Remember that film you saw in science with that bear sloshing through the river to pull out those fat salmon? Boy, did that bear ever look scared."

The grizzly approached the spot where I had filled the pop can. It sniffed at my footprints and then searched the air. I continued to back into the lake.

The water that washed around my legs was freezing. My calves tightened in protest.

The wind blew sharply across the open water and flakes of wet snow danced angrily in gusts. The grizzly stopped at the water's edge and dropped its head. It peered across the water, searching for me.

I glanced around. In the increasing darkness I could see nothing but the black surface of Hay Lake. There was nowhere to run.

The bear growled, a low, seeking noise that rippled across the water.

"Go away," I murmured.

"Good plan," my mind mocked. "Plead with the thing. That'll make it leave."

The bear edged forward, making tiny splashes as its front paws entered the water. It snorted angrily and then sniffed the air.

"Go away," I mumbled again.

And the bear did.

With a huff of frustration, it wheeled around and vanished noiselessly back into the bush.

The shivering moved from my legs and soon my whole body was racked with violent tremors. I fought the urge to collapse and made my left foot move in front of the right. I had to make it back to the shore.

It was painful trudging through the cold lake. The chill of the water sent needles of pain deep into my legs. The wind blew the wet snow against my cheeks.

I had to get the water back to Doc Raghbir. The doc was hurt bad. I wasn't sure if giving him water would save his life. I just didn't know. But I couldn't take the chance. I couldn't wait here by the water for the police to rescue me as well. Doc Raghbir was counting on me.

But I also knew that when I slipped past those willows into the darkness of the trees, I'd probably run smack into the grizzly again. Probably? Heck, I was fooling myself. That monster was in there and the chance was more than probable that it would find me.

I reached the shore and scrambled wetly onto the brown grass. "Come on Nicky, baby," my mind rationalized. "Just stay here.

Elvis and the cops are on their way. They'll reach the doc before you do."

"What if they don't?" I muttered to myself. "What if he's still waiting for a truck? What if help doesn't come for another hour? Or more. It's getting cold. I have to keep the doc warm."

I forged into the willows, holding the pop can in front of me. The gloom turned the bush into a grey-black mask and willow branches snapped at my face. My body had stopped shivering but a cold claw gripped my leg muscles. In the middle of the swamp spruce, the grey sky melted into the treetops. Clumps of caribou moss twisted into bearlike shapes behind the trunks. I pushed forward.

The muskeg gurgled and belched with my footsteps. I couldn't be much farther from the clearing. I was going to make it.

The spruce thinned and I jogged into the clearing. The wind lashed the snow into my face, but I didn't mind.

I'd made it. "Take that, you stupid bear!" I called out as I ran faster.

The coldness and discomfort had vanished. I'd faced the bear, not once, but twice. And I was still here!

Everything was going to be all right. I'd outsmarted the grizzly. I was going to get water for the doc. The cops would rescue him soon and I'd get taken home where it was warm and the only thing I had to worry about was Gerry Walmsley. My dad would be so surprised. And wait until I phoned my mom in Calgary.

Without thinking about it, I let out a holler, a cheer of victory.

I reached the poplar saplings and saw the path that Elvis and I had beaten to the plane. I charged into the trail, scampering over the broken branches. For some reason, I was able to move more quickly toward the doc than when I had left. I figured it must have been the incredible high that I felt. I remembered my mom telling me about somebody who felt so good he was walking two steps off the ground. That was just the way I felt.

I didn't think that I was moving faster because the trail was wider.

In the increasing dusk, I almost bumped into the tail of the plane. "I'm here, Doc," I called. "I've got some water."

I scrambled around the side of the plane and froze. The grizzly was sniffing at the door of the cockpit. I dropped the pop can. It landed with a dull thud on the ground.

The *gleeze* turned to me, snarled angrily and lifted its upper lip to display those sharp white teeth.

CHAPTER 9

"GET away from him!" I screamed.

I looked at the gun, still propped against the side of the plane. It was so close. But it was closer to the grizzly. If I tried to get it, I'd be near enough to kiss that monster. I had to do something else. So I yelled.

"Get away from him!"

I wasn't being brave. There is no such thing as bravery when you're facing something that can kill you with a mere brush of its arm. But I was desperate. I had to get the bear away from Doc Raghbir.

"Leave him alone!" I shouted, and the bear's shoulders quivered as if it had been startled.

"You big, stupid fur-face! Get lost!" I hollered.

"Good words," my mind coached. "Keep shouting at it and you won't have to think about how scared you are."

The terror I'd felt at the lake had been magnified ten times. It clutched my insides in a vise grip. My pulse thudded so strongly in my temples that I could hear it.

The bear remained unmoving, resting its gigantic body on the plane and watching me as if it was amused.

"You no-good scum!" I continued. "I'm gonna rip out your eyes and stomp on them!"

The animal seemed suddenly bored. It pushed away from the Cessna and glided gracefully onto all fours. Then it tilted its head.

"Go for it!" my mind urged. "The thing figures you're a loony tune. Wild animals never eat loony tunes. It's a proven fact. Prove to it how crazy you really are."

I began to bounce up and down and yell and scream. "Get outta here, stupid!" I waved my hands above my head.

The beast backed up a step. Now it looked confused. Maybe, just maybe, I had spooked it. This just might work out.

"I'm so scared I may drop dead of a heart attack, unless you move your hairy rear out of here!" I yelled.

The *gleeze* looked to its right and then quickly back at me.

"It's looking for a way out, Nicky," my mind cheered.

"If you don't leave right now, I'll make you go out with my old girlfriend! She'll belch in your face!" I jumped up and down on the smashed saplings. Then I began to scream. My shrill howls hurt my throat. But I continued screaming until my voice was raw and I began to cough.

"Please go away," I pleaded gruffly.

The animal tensed its shoulders and started to growl. A deep, sickly sound oozed from its lungs and filled the bush.

"That's not a good sign, Nicky," my mind observed.

"This has got to work!" I tried hollering again. "If it doesn't, I'm bear food!"

Yeah, it had to work. Not only for me, but for the doc. If I didn't succeed in spooking the monster, then it would get Doc Raghbir ...

The animal released such a chilling yowl that I stopped jumping and hollering and stared at it. The blood pounded through my head. "I'm impressed," I croaked.

"It didn't work," my mind said. "Time for Plan B."

Plan B, I thought. Plan B is total panic!

The bear pounced at me with incredible speed and agility. One moment a resting hulk and the next, a blur of motion.

It would have had me, if I wasn't well into Plan B. As it jumped, I was scrambling behind the tail of the plane. A massive paw missed my head by a half second and landed against the sheet metal with a vicious smack.

I scampered on my hands and knees along the other side of the fuselage. The grizzly momentarily thrown off balance by my disappearance, rounded the tail section in a yowling fury.

The shorn trees stopped my progress. I pulled at them, trying to put distance between King Kong and me, but they were too tangled. I twisted around and saw the beast ripping at the same uprooted trees to get to me.

The bear was the only thing I could see. The darkness melted around it and it became the only thing in the world.

"Play dead!" my mind ordered. "If you play dead it'll go away."

Play dead, I thought? Play? I am dead.

The bear charged at me and instinctively I grabbed my knees and buried my head in my chest. I waited for the monster to tear me to pieces.

Nature must have a way of protecting our thoughts from accepting the horrible, because I passed the point of fear. As I lay on those ripped aspens, clenched in my babylike position, I became detached from what was happening. I waited for the creature to come, waited for that beast to smash its terrible claws on me. I wondered, curiously, what it would feel like to be clawed and chewed on. How long would it take to die?

There was a violent smash on my back that pushed the wind from me. Then I was hit again, hard, on my side. I couldn't breathe. The bear was pawing at me. I wondered if I was bleeding. I couldn't feel anything but the sensation of suffocating. I wanted to stretch out to regain my breath, but I tightened my grip on my knees. I waited for another bash.

It didn't happen.

I heard a snuffling sound behind my head and then a wave of stench dug at my nostrils. It was the grizzly's breath. It was sniffing me.

The snuffling grew louder, a snorting, bubbly noise. The bear's snout rubbed against the back of my head and across my hair. It rested briefly against my ear, leaving a deposit of warm mucus. Then it exhaled stinking breath around my face. Gently it nuzzled my cheek, the way a friendly dog would, pushing at me as if it was trying to get me to wake up.

At that point I snapped out of my trance and the terror again exploded in my brain. But the fear made me think. Maybe that article was right. Maybe the bear thought I was dead and that was enough to make it lose interest. Maybe I still had a chance.

The bear nudged me again, pushing urgently at my cheek.

I remained in a ball.

The bear shoved its snout into the small of my back and bulldozed me against the broken trees. Then the grizzly used its head as a shovel and lifted me into the air. I landed savagely on the sharp ends of the shorn trunks.

The bear grunted and sprayed me with thick saliva. A branch or small trunk was sticking to my side and I wanted to roll over. The bear released an angry, frustrated growl and suddenly my consciousness was a layer of pain at the back of my head. And then I remember nothing.

I'm not sure how long I was unconscious. It couldn't have been more than a minute or two because there was still a little light behind the clouds when I opened my eyes. A moment passed before I realized where I was. I remained unmoving, waiting for clues of the bear's presence. Then I twisted my head slowly to look behind me. There was no bear. It was gone.

I staggered to my knees with the bush swimming in front of me. I had to concentrate to stop the bush from spinning. The back of my neck and head ached and I rubbed them gingerly. My hair was coated with something sticky. When I looked at my hand, I knew it was blood.

I swore and got to my feet. The bear had swatted me in anger. Because it thought I was dead, it had bashed me in the back of the head in frustration. But I was alive.

"Three times in one day, Nicky," my mind said. "Nobody is gonna believe it. You don't even believe it, do you?"

I stumbled against the side of the plane when a wave of dizziness broke between my ears. The doc! I had to see the doc. Still supporting myself on the fuselage, I staggered around the plane.

The *gleeze* watched me with the same curiosity it had shown when I'd appeared earlier. I guess I should have figured that it would go back to the doc after losing interest in me. It had managed to pry the door half open and it returned to its chore, ignoring me as if I was no longer worth any effort.

A red mist filled my sight. Four times in one day! Enough was enough! I reached down and grabbed a thick, shorn trunk. Then I charged, screaming, at the bear. The bear watched me stupidly as I ran at it. It stood resting on the plane as I swung the trunk behind me and brought it down with a vicious thud on the bridge of its nose. The wood split and the bear howled in surprise and pain.

I heaved the stump over my head and brought it down again, but the bear had vanished. It was running down the trail and out of the bush. The swing at the empty air threw me off balance and I fell to the ground.

It was dark now, almost night. I pulled myself to the planes's door and eased in beside Doc Raghbir. He was conscious, staring at me with his good eye.

"Nich'las," he mumbled. "Nich'las?"

"Damn right," I smiled at him.

"Bear," he stuttered.

"Right again," I continued to smile. "Biggest bear in the whole world. And, boy, did it give me a hard time. But I bashed a home run right in its nose and sent it off. That's one bear that isn't going to mess with me again." I was giddy. My legs were cold and I knew I was shivering but I didn't care.

"Warer."

"I hope so," I said as I went back to the front of the plane and groped around for the pop can. It was resting almost on its side, but it was still half full of water. I returned to the doc and tilted the can by his lips. A dribble ran down his chin, but he drank thirstily.

"Thank you," he said. His voice sounded stronger.

"You're welcome," I grinned. "Is there anything else you want?"

"Out of here." He tried to return my grin through a swollen face.

"My friend has gone to get help," I told him. "It won't be long now."

As if on cue, the air thudded with the vibrations of helicopter engines. The sky was immediately filled with spotlights and the bush returned to daylight.

"Speak of the devil," I chuckled.

In less than a minute, I was being helped away from the door of the plane by a paramedic. An RCMP took my arm and directed me to the pathway and out of the bush. "Wait here," he told me. "We'll want to talk to you in a moment. You've done a great thing."

Elvis strode beside me. "Hey, Nicholas!" he said. "I got a ride in the chopper."

"Terrific."

The cop smiled at us and went back into the bush.

"Is the doc still okay?" Elvis asked.

"Oh, yeah. He's gonna be fine, I think."

"I'm sorry I wasn't faster. When I got to the Zama Road, I tried to flag down a pickup, but it kept on going. I had to wait ten minutes for another truck. I stood in the middle of the road to make sure it stopped. The guys had a mobile and we got the cops right away. They flew a helicopter to get me and then on to you."

"Terrific," I said again.

"Anything happen here?" he asked.

"Not really," I said. "I ran into the grizzly again. By the lake. When I went to get the doc some water."

"You're kidding!" he gasped. "What did you do?"

"Took a swim," I told him.

"And it went away?"

"Kind of."

"What?" he demanded curiously.

"It came back to try to get the doc, but I hit it over the nose with a stick after it took a swipe at the back of my head."

"What?" He stared at me with a stupid, open-mouthed grin and I had to smile.

"My head feels like it's going to burst and my legs are so cold I think they're going numb. Do you mind if I rest on your shoulder?"

I put my hand on his shoulder and supported my weight. Elvis was shouting for help, calling to the cops, but it sounded very far away. Strong hands were supporting my other arm and I no longer wanted to stand up. I'm not sure if I passed out or simply went to sleep.

CHAPTER 10

ELVIS walked into my room in the High Level hospital with suspicious bulges beneath his jacket.

"Hey, Elvis," I said, jumping from my chair and tossing the Spiderman comic aside. "Am I ever glad to see you."

"Same," he said. "Your dad called me this morning to say that you were allowed to have visitors today."

He unzipped his jacket. Two bags of ketchup potato chips fell onto the bed. Then he reached inside the coat and pulled out two cans of Cherry Coke. "Figured you'd be hungry by now." He threw one of the bags of chips at me.

"I don't really like this stuff."

"Eat it anyway," he scolded, climbing onto the hospital bed. "What kind of kid doesn't like junk food?"

I sat down, ripping the top off the bag and wincing at the odour of simulated ketchup. "I'm getting out this aft," I told him. "Probably just before supper. Dr. Chiou says I can go back to school tomorrow if I want."

"Great. Your dad told me that you were doing all right. He `said that you had a wicked bruise on your neck and you needed a couple of stitches in the cuts on your head."

"And sore ribs," I added. "Other than that I feel fine."

"Yeah, you look great. How come they kept you in for three days?"

"I dunno," I shrugged. "They said that I'd be under a great stress and sometimes people went into shock, whatever that is. Doc Chiou said that it's a pretty standard thing when you get a whack on the head."

"Two days off school, anyway." Elvis shoved a handful of chips into his face. "How's Doc Raghbir?"

"One of the nurses said that he was doing great," I told him. "You know they took him to Edmonton right away? Seems he had a bad concussion and a few bruises, but nothing really serious. Doc Chiou thinks he may be back at work in a couple of weeks."

"My dad heard that there was something wrong with the engine of the doc's plane. He was turning back to Rainbow when the engine cut. The wind blew him out to Hay Lake. That's why we found him there," Elvis explained as he pulled the tab on the Cherry Coke. He swallowed the contents of half the can. "You want yours yet?"

"The stuff is so sweet. It's like drinking pancake syrup."

"Never tried that," he said seriously.

"But now you probably will," I grimaced.

"Hey, did you know that you're a big hero at school?"

Elvis went on. "All the girls are gonna want to dance with you at the next sock hop."

"A hero? Why do they think that?"

"Come on," Elvis laughed. "You practising being humble or something? You saved the doc by wrestling a one tonne grizzly bear."

"Elvis, I'm no hero."

"Yeah, you are," he nodded. "You scared the bear away and probably saved the doc's life."

"But I wasn't being brave."

"Enjoy it," he grinned. "The cops think you're a hero. They're gonna give us some kind of award thing."

"Award?"

"Boy, are you being dense." He crunched the chips noisily. "A medal or something. For saving the doc."

"Gosh."

"Gosh? You did a brave thing staying by Doc Raghbir when that bear was gunning for him. Like it or not, lots of people are going to want to get close to you."

I took a bite of a chip. It was awful.

"You know," Elvis winked, "I think Sandra Travis wants to get real close."

"Pardon?"

"Well, she keeps asking me how you are and when you're getting out," he explained.

"She does?"

"What's the matter? Don't you like the idea of Sandra asking about you?"

I shook my head. "No way. Gerry Walmsley is mad enough at me already."

"I wouldn't worry about Gerry anymore," Elvis said. "Like I said, you're a hero. Even Gerry isn't going to beat up a hero."

"I'm not convinced." I shook my head.

"I am," Elvis asserted. "Gerry even asked me when you were getting out."

"That's because he wants to know when he can kill me."

Elvis chuckled. "Wrong again. He invited you and me to a party at his place next Friday. He wanted to know if you were going to be able to make it."

"You're kidding?"

"For guys like Walmsley, it's important to

112

be with all the new stuff that's happening," Elvis pointed out. "Right now we're that new stuff."

"I can't believe it."

"No doubt Sandra will be there," Elvis winked again. "And that's a big improvement over look-and-see nostrils."

"You know, Elvis, for the past two days I've been sitting here thinking about what I was going to do when I met Walmsley again."

"Now you don't have to run away."

"That's what I was thinking about," I told him. "I was thinking about all the times I've run away. I'm not going to run away from anybody or anything again."

"You were willing to fight Walmsley?" He stopped chewing for a moment.

I nodded. "I figured he would beat the tar out of me, but I wasn't going to beg him not to. I was going to fight him with whatever strength I had. He'd destroy me, but he'd have to earn it."

"Sounds like a different Nicholas."

I ate another chip. "Do you know what happened to that bear?"

"They caught him." Elvis sprayed chip bits over the bed. "Uncle Wild Dog told me that the Fish and Wildlife guys went in and shot him with one of those tranquilizer darts. Then they strapped him to the bottom of a helicopter, flew a hundred kilometres into the bush and let him go. That monster won't bother anyone else again."

"I was wondering what they'd do. I was afraid they'd kill it."

Elvis scrunched his face. "That would bother you?"

"Sure," I told him. "It didn't deserve to die."

Elvis just shrugged and finished his pop. He looked at my bag of ketchup chips. "You gonna eat those?"

"No." I offered them to him. "My dad has taken a couple of days off work, you know."

"Your dad? Your dad is like mine. They work eight days a week."

"It's kind of funny really," I told him. "Funny in a strange way. He's almost like a different person. Yesterday he sat here all day and we talked. We've never done that before."

"What did you talk about?"

"About him and my mom. And about his job. And his drinking. And him and me. About everything, really."

"No kidding? How come you think he did that?"

"I don't know," I said. "He told me that getting the call from the cops telling him I'd been attacked by a bear really shook him up.

114

And that until he saw me in the hospital, he was afraid I was gonna die."

"Must have been scary for him."

"Then he said stuff that I didn't really understand. That when he thought he might lose me, he promised himself that he'd take better care of me."

"It sounds like he's feeling guilty," Elvis said.

"But he didn't say it that straightforward," I explained. "That's what I think he was trying to say. My dad says things in a kind of roundabout way."

"Some people are like that."

"You know, running into the bear was the best thing that ever happened to me."

"A bashed-up head is good for you?"

"No," I told him. "I don't mean that. I'm just saying that the whole experience was a big step for me. Wading after those ducks and trying to clean them. And trying that snuff. I'd never have done that before."

Elvis laughed. "I wish you could have seen your face when you swallowed that snuff juice."

"But the bear," I went on. "Facing the bear those four times. That changed me. It made me realize that I can do something about the problems I get myself into."

"I'm losing you," Elvis confessed.

"It made me realize I'm not a wimp."

"Hey, I knew that," he grinned. "You had the act down perfect, but I knew that you weren't really a nerd."

"You did?"

"Sure," he nodded. "You didn't change, Nicholas. You just acted more like yourself."

"But before I was afraid of things. Afraid of guys like Walmsley."

"And you're not now?" Elvis said. "If you're not scared of tough guys, then you've changed into a jerk."

"But I used to be more scared than other people."

"No," Elvis shook his head. "You used to think about being scared more than other people. When you faced the bear you thought more about doing something than how afraid you were."

I leaned back in the chair and smiled. "Maybe that's what I was trying to say."

Elvis threw the empty chip bag into the garbage and picked up my Cherry Coke. "Okay if I finish this?"

"Sure."

"I gotta go," he said. "The bell is going to ring soon. By the way, next week we're having a t-dance on the reserve and you're invited."

"A what?" I asked.

116

"A t-dance. It's sort of a party. I think once upon a time it was a way to honour our ancestors, but I'm not sure about that. Now it's a big dance. The old people get together and beat skin drums and tell stories of brave deeds. This time they'll probably tell the story of what happened to us in the bush."

I thought about that. Me, in a story. Elvis, the doc, the bear and me in a story.

"Really? You mean we'll become part of a story?"

"That's how legends are made," he grinned. He paused at the door for a moment. "Thanks again for helping me out when I froze."

"I thought we'd sorted that out."

"Yeah." He made a faint smile.

"Elvis?"

"Uh-huh?"

"Why were we really following that bear? You were hunting it, weren't you?"

He nodded his head slowly. "I wanted to get it. I wanted to shoot the thing and become a big deal on the reserve." He paused. "I guess I learned something about myself out there, too. I'm sorry you got hurt because of me."

"If we hadn't followed the bear, we wouldn't have found the doc," I pointed out.

He smiled again. "Take care, Nicholas."

117

As the door hissed shut, I wondered about the bear, where it was and what it was doing. Was it nursing a sore nose? It would be hibernating soon. I wondered if bears dreamt when they hibernated. Would it dream of Elvis and me?

I was going to have to learn about stuff like that. I was going to have to start going into the bush more often. After all, I lived in the middle of it. I should know more about it.

Yeah, I was going to have to do a lot more stuff. And suddenly, I was laughing to myself.

"Go for it, Nicky," my inner voice cheered. "Go for it."